# ALBERT STRIDEMORE'S LOCKDOWN DISCOVERIES

## Surprising what you uncover when you've time to dig

# Chick Yuill

instant
ap□stle

First published in Great Britain in 2020

Instant Apostle
The Barn
1 Watford House Lane
Watford
Herts
WD17 1BJ

British Library Cataloguing-in-Publication Data

A catalogue record for this book is available from the British Library.

This book and all other Instant Apostle books are available from Instant Apostle:

Website: www.instantapostle.com

Email: info@instantapostle.com

ISBN 978-1-912726-33-2

Printed in Great Britain.

# Acknowledgements

The characters in this novel are fictional. And, while the action is set in Manchester, most of the specific locations are imagined. It is, however, a tale that plays out and was actually written during a time that is all too real – the period of lockdown in the UK between March and August 2020. My research has been my own experience of those days, augmented by close attention to news reports in the broadcast and print media and frequent recourse to numerous relevant websites. To the best of my knowledge, all references to real events in matters such as dates and numbers are accurate.

I had only just completed my previous novel at the end of March 2020 and had no intention of immediately starting on a new project. One novel a year is more than enough for me! But for some reason the name of Albert Stridemore came into my mind and the character of the man began to take shape.

This book is the result. I am greatly indebted to Nicki Copeland and the team at Instant Apostle for bringing it to publication so quickly. I also need to record my debt to Sheila Jacobs, my eagle-eyed editor, whose constructive criticisms have made it a better book than it would otherwise have been. Any factual errors are those of the author. Most of all, I must record my heartfelt thanks to my ever-patient wife who not only allowed me to embark on another five months of writing, but also gave me her unstinting support and encouragement.

Finally, I dedicate this book to the memory of all those who lost their lives to Covid-19, those who devoted their lives in service on the frontline, and those who sacrificed their lives to save others. It comes with my prayer that they will have discovered the great truth to which this story seeks to point.

# Contents

# Contents

What else is the epidemic but a fire which instead of consuming wood and straw devours life and body …

Therefore I shall ask God mercifully to protect us. Then I shall fumigate, help purify the air, administer medicine, and take it. I shall avoid places and persons where my presence is not needed in order not to become contaminated and thus perchance infect and pollute others, and so cause their death as a result of my negligence.

If God should wish to take me, he will surely find me and I have done what he has expected of me and so I am not responsible for either my own death or the death of others.

If my neighbour needs me, however, I shall not avoid place or person but will go freely …

Everyone should prepare in time and get ready for death by going to confession and taking the sacrament once every week or fortnight. He should become reconciled with his neighbour and make his will so that if the Lord knocks and he departs before a pastor or chaplain can arrive, he has provided for his soul, has left nothing undone, and has committed himself to God.

*Martin Luther: Whether One May Flee From A Deadly Plague*

# 1
## 3rd January 2020
## What's in a Name?

Albert Stridemore's neighbours on the Irmingshawe estate would often observe that never had a man been more appropriately christened. 'He really *is* an Albert,' they would say to each other as he passed with a curt nod of his head and a brief greeting – never usually more than 'G'morning' or 'Afternoon' or 'Evening', depending on the time of the day – as he made his way to or from his allotment, where he'd spent much of his time since his retirement ten years before our story begins. Their comments were not in any way intended as a reference to the etymology of his name. Few if any of them of them were sufficiently schooled in ancient Germanic languages to know that Albert was derived from two words meaning *noble* and *bright*, though there was a certain dignity and alertness in his upright bearing that would have rendered both of those adjectives appropriate to describe his appearance and character. It was just that 'Albert' had such an old-fashioned ring to it. They certainly couldn't conceive of anybody calling their son Albert today! It was a name that conjured up for them images of black and

13

white films and music halls and British Tommys going off to war and vintage cars belching out clouds of exhaust fumes as they trundled along at twenty miles an hour.

And the man himself seemed to embody an aura of decades long past. He dressed in a manner that made no concession to the changing fashions and increasing informality of the twenty-first century. Even on the warmest of days, and whatever his intended destination, he would set off from home wearing a shirt and tie, a tweed sports jacket, grey flannels and a stout pair of good-quality leather brogue shoes. When the weather was wet, as it frequently is in that part of England, he would supplement his attire and protect himself from the elements with a light-brown belted overcoat and a flat cap pulled down over his eyes to shield them from the rain. In the view of his neighbours, everything about him announced that he was indeed an Albert.

His surname, however, amused and fascinated them even more. It certainly wasn't common in Manchester. In fact, none of them could ever recall encountering another family with that name. But they all agreed that Stridemore was perfect for him. Normal folk like themselves might saunter aimlessly down the road when they wanted just to stretch their legs, or rush madly to the shops when they suddenly remembered something they'd forgotten. No one had ever seen Albert walk like that. When he stepped out of his house each morning, he neither hesitated nor hurried. He would lock his door, put his key carefully into his jacket pocket, turn smartly to face the street, look to the left and to the right, take a long, deep breath, pull back his shoulders and draw himself up to his full height of just

14

over six feet, before striding out purposefully at a pace from which he seldom deviated. And that characteristic striding gait seemed to set him a little apart from his neighbours, giving him the air of a man on a mission, a man with something important to do, a man who understood the value of time and the need to use it wisely.

Those of his neighbours who'd known him for more than a decade assumed that his apparent preoccupation with the task in hand and his determination to step out boldly wherever he was heading had, in large measure, been shaped by the occupation he'd followed for most of his working life. Until his retirement in 2010, Albert had been a postman, respected among his colleagues at the sorting office and appreciated by the householders on his round for his commitment to the job. In forty years, whatever the weather, he'd never missed a day's work through illness and never failed to deliver the right letters to the right house at the right time. His efficiency and his local knowledge were such that on more than one occasion he'd been recommended for promotion to an administrative role. It was an offer he'd always dismissed out of hand, insisting that no increase in his wages and no elevation in his professional status could ever be sufficient to compensate for sacrificing the privilege of combining work and pleasure by walking purposefully in the fresh air day after day.

But there were others who'd lived there for much longer, who remembered the day Albert Stridemore had moved into the area, and who suspected that there were deeper forces at play that had made him the man he was. At first, the arrival of the tall, shy, young man with the two-year-old toddler in the summer of 1970 had given rise to suspicious questions about his past and whispered speculation as to the whereabouts of the child's mother. Situated on the opposite side of a busy road from the Irmingshawe Park with its expanse of woodland and open stretches of grass, the 'Shawe, as the council estate was known by its residents, was considered to be one of the jewels in the crown of the local authority's rental properties. To be allocated a terraced house on the 'Shawe – or even one of a handful of semi-detached dwellings, if you were very lucky – was to be the envy of those who had to settle for less well-appointed dwellings in the city's housing stock. And there were some among those favoured residents – a handful of zealous and outspoken, if self-appointed, guardians of the 'Shawe's working-class respectability – who were fearful that its reputation might be endangered by the presence of a single man with a young child and no wife.

Albert Stridemore's regular employment, tidy front garden, smartly painted front door and well-mannered young son, however, soon earned the trust and respect of the great majority of his neighbours and silenced the ill-informed gossips. He quickly became a valued member of the community. And the more discerning of his neighbours recognised that, though they knew nothing of his past, they were fortunate to have a man of his calibre in their midst.

Now in his mid-seventies, Albert was not a man much given to nostalgia. He never pined for a golden age when the sun always shone and people could leave their front doors unlocked and children always spoke politely to their parents. He knew too much about life's trials and tribulations to view the past through rose-coloured spectacles. The only time he compared the present unfavourably with what had gone before was when he happened to come across one of his successors in the postal service delivering letters. He was not at all impressed by those who put forward the case that today's postman is just as recognisable and a whole lot more comfortable in shorts and a polo shirt emblazoned with the logo of the Royal Mail. The job, he would contend, had a lot more dignity when those who delivered the mail were dressed smartly in a uniform that marked them out as servants of the Crown.

If he was far from being the most loquacious resident of the 'Shawe, he was certainly not unfriendly or aloof. Albert was on good terms with his neighbours, and he was happy to be a member of the residents' association, even serving two successive three-year terms as an active and effective chair of the group. He'd never remarried, much to the disappointment of more than a few single women and younger widows across the years. Noting his smart appearance and reliable employment, they'd considered him to be excellent husband material. He'd politely but firmly spurned their sometimes not-so-subtle advances, seeming to feel no need for female companionship in his life. His only son had left home in the late eighties and he'd lived alone in apparent contentment since then. And now in retirement, his tastes were simple, his needs were few, and he was grateful for his pensions that allowed him to live comfortably and indulge his passion for tending his allotment and cultivating his vegetables. He asked nothing more from life.

On this chilly but sunny afternoon, as he made his way home through Irmingshawe Park at the beginning of another year, he felt at peace with the world and with himself. Whatever he was hearing on the news these days about strange and possibly deadly viruses in faraway places was unlikely to have any significant effect on him or his neighbours on the 'Shawe. And, though no one else was aware of it and he himself felt no need to mark the occasion with any celebration, today was his seventy-fifth birthday. It was just another milestone on the journey of life to be briefly noted in passing and then left behind. He felt fit and active and, barring some unexpected accident, he saw no reason that he should not continue walking briskly and cultivating his allotment lovingly for a few more years. While still in his early thirties, the warrior king Alexander the Great was said to have wept because there were no worlds left for him to conquer. But halfway through his eighth decade, with his life attuned to the recurring rhythms of the seasons, Albert Stridemore, retired postman and active allotment-keeper, was grateful that the world was unlikely to hold any more surprises for him.

# 2
# 24th March 2020
# Lockdown

Albert Stridemore washed his hands under the standing tap just in front of his shed and dried them thoroughly with a towel he kept hanging from a hook on the back of the door for precisely that purpose. He poured the tea from his flask into a bright yellow mug decorated with the words *Growing stuff is good for you* and took one of his cheese sandwiches out of the stainless-steel lunchbox that he'd carried with him almost every day for longer than he could remember. He set them down beside the newspaper lying on the workbench running up the side of the shed and shuffled the old folding metal chair to the door where he could sit and take a long look around his allotment while he ate and drank. He loved this place – this plot of fertile land that was as much his home as his house on the Irmingshawe estate – more than anywhere else in all the world. And he treasured the perfect combination of solitude and company it afforded him. Here he had the freedom to be alone with his thoughts while still appreciating the opportunity for conversation with likeminded allotment-holders who might offer or seek advice on their shared passion for growing things from the rich, moist soil under their feet. He measured the passing of time, not by the ticking of a clock or by marking off the dates on a calendar fixed to the wall, but by the tasks he carried out here hour after hour, day after day, week after week, month after month.

The festivities of Christmas and New Year were for him, at worst, an annoying interruption to his labour of love and, at best, nothing more than a necessary prelude to getting on with the real purpose of his life. By ten o'clock in the morning of 2nd January each year he was back here, happily unlocking the door of his shed. It was nothing more elaborate than a simple shack with just enough space for his tools and a place for him to sit when he felt like taking a rest. But he was proud of it, having put it together with his own hands out of wood he'd salvaged from a nearby derelict building. The old aircraft factory had stood no more than 150 yards from the allotments until it had been targeted by the Luftwaffe on consecutive nights in late December 1940 in what older Mancunians still referred to as the 'Christmas Blitz'. Despite the complaints of people living in the area, the ruined structure had been left until the council finally razed it to the ground to make space for a proposed though never completed housing development the year after Albert had taken possession of his allotment in 1990. He was no builder, but the shed kept his tools safe and sheltered him from the rain when he stopped for a cup of tea. And, to his surprise, it was still standing nearly thirty years after its construction.

At the beginning of each year, he'd throw open the door, carefully check that everything was in good order and joyfully resume the routine he loved so much. Invariably he would begin by examining his stored vegetables for signs of rot and emptying the bags of potatoes that were leaning against the wall, making sure to remove any slugs that might have hidden themselves in the cosy darkness of the hessian sacks. When he got to the point of chitting the potatoes, he knew that the year had really begun. It was impossible to explain to anyone else the surge of anticipation that always went through him when he placed the tubers 'eyes up' in a dozen old egg boxes that he'd begged from the shop where he bought the food that he couldn't grow for himself. He knew from long experience that within just a couple of weeks they would develop the little shoots that would mean they were ready for burying in the ground. The weather was normally still too cold to allow him to plant anything out of doors, but the rest of the month could profitably be filled by building his runner bean trenches, making sure there were no cracked panes of glass in the greenhouse, and repairing the wooden-sided cold frames that he painstakingly patched up each year to provide the perfect nursery for his summer cauliflowers, a vegetable he swore tasted all the better for its early start to life.

February was sometimes the most difficult month of the year for Albert. Snow and frost, or more often just cold sleet and rain, left him at the mercy of the elements and limited what could be done. But apart from a handful of days over the years, when the weather had been just too bad for him to venture out of doors, he always made his

21

way to the allotment. If nothing else, he could check that no damage had been inflicted by the high winds or, as occasionally happened, by vandals whose destructive urges he could never comprehend. Even in Manchester, however, the weather was sometimes sufficiently dry and mild to allow him to begin planting outdoors under a cloche to ensure he'd have a healthy crop of broad beans, peas and artichokes by May or June. And as the days brightened a little and the allotment began to show the early evidence of his hard work, his spirits would lift and his heart would beat a little faster in the knowledge that spring was just around the corner.

March, despite the unpredictability of the weather, always meant a flurry of activity. Row upon row of parsnips, carrots, radishes, turnips, Brussels sprouts, spring onions and celery could be directly sown. Albert would bury the seeds in the ground and wait with an unshakeable faith for the annual miracle of growth that would explode into a generous harvest later in the year.

But it was April that he loved more than any other month. Even though a sudden and unexpected cold snap could take the most experienced gardener by surprise and lay siege to all his back-breaking toil, it was the time when the earth stirred into life and the soil warmed and the days began to lengthen noticeably. Spring had come at last. It was, he always said with a knowing smile, 'the season of hoeing and sowing and growing'. Unwelcome weeds were gently and carefully removed to ensure the unhindered growth of runner beans and dwarf beans and climbing beans and borlotti beans – beans everywhere! And if the day became chilly or his joints grew stiff from kneeling and bending, there was always the relief of retreating to the relative warmth and comfort of the greenhouse where tomatoes and peppers and aubergines required the loving attention of the amateur but expert horticulturist.

But on this afternoon, just a week from the start of the month to which he'd always looked forward with such growing anticipation, Albert's emotions were mixed and his thoughts were in turmoil. Ten minutes after he'd set them out, his mug of tea was still half full and his cheese sandwich remained uneaten as he tried to take stock of things. The allotment was as wonderful a place to him as ever it had been. *But everything else was different.* Life had suddenly changed. Even before the turn of the year he'd been vaguely aware of brief reports on the news about the emergence of a strange new virus in the Chinese city of Wuhan – a place that neither he nor anyone else he knew had ever heard of. In four decades of life as a postman, he'd never once delivered a letter that had come from Wuhan!

Nobody had seemed to be particularly worried about the virus. It had all seemed such a long way away, and chances were, everyone had agreed, that it would be similar to the SARS outbreak a few years earlier – confined to a distant region of the world and unlikely to have any real impact on the everyday lives of folk in this country. Gradually, however, the items on the news had become more frequent, the newspaper articles lengthened, and the tone had become more serious and urgent. By the end of January, he was reading and hearing about people who'd returned from China being tracked down by the authorities and put in strict quarantine for fourteen days. Even more concerning, he'd seen something about two members of the same family having tested positive for the disease and ending up in hospital in Newcastle. That was a lot nearer Manchester than Wuhan! The whole thing was becoming much more concerning.

Throughout February, as the flow of information gathered momentum and reports of new infections became more common, things began to move at a pace that alarmed even the hitherto easy-going residents of the Irmingshawe estate. There was a discernible change in the atmosphere of the place. The Patel family's much-valued corner shop had sold out of toilet rolls and hand-wash dispensers several times already. And Albert had overheard his neighbours talking about 'the virus' to each other in the street on his daily trips to and from his allotment. People who previously had shown only a passing interest in national and international affairs were discussing the need for a new vaccine to counter the disease or offering their opinions on how best to protect themselves from infection. He even overheard Mrs Armitage, whose interaction with her neighbours was normally confined to voicing her complaints about teenage boys playing football in the street and who was not normally given to using words of ancient Greek derivation, articulating her fears regarding the 'draconian measures' the government might impose on its citizens if things got any worse. Clearly, ordinary people were taking the situation seriously.

By the beginning of March, it seemed that everybody had assimilated two new medical terms into their vocabulary – *coronavirus* and *Covid-19*. Few people could have explained precisely what the words meant, but they were usually uttered with a worried expression and followed by a shaking of the head and a sharp intake of breath. It quickly became apparent that their fears were not unfounded. Within a few days, the handful of cases became hundreds and word of the first deaths began to be solemnly announced on the evening news. Experts speculated that while the official number of those suffering from the disease was still relatively small in proportion to the population, in all probability thousands more had been infected. And though most of those who had succumbed might have suffered only mild symptoms, or even none at all, early studies suggested worryingly that it was highly likely that they could still be capable of transmitting the illness to others. Towards the middle of the month daily press briefings began on television, people were advised against travelling to other countries, and there were dire warnings that, unless stricter measures were put in place, the death toll could reach as high as 250,000.

Albert Stridemore had been born in the last months of the Second World War. He'd been rocked to sleep to the accompaniment of his mother's soothing voice repeating the words, 'Keep Calm and Carry On'. He'd been schooled from childhood in the British virtue of always keeping a stiff upper lip in every circumstance. But even Albert was growing nervous.

And just last night his nervousness had changed to a degree of annoyance that took him by surprise and threatened to become an irrational anger. The streets of the

Irmingshawe estate had been unusually quite in the evening as most of its residents settled themselves in front of their televisions to hear the Prime Minister's statement on the measures the government had decided to take. Albert didn't have a fixed allegiance to any particular political party and usually cast his vote on the basis of which of the local candidates he considered the better man or woman and the most likely to represent the needs of their constituents faithfully and effectively. And he did acknowledge a definite bias in himself against the man looking out at him from his television screen. He admitted to being 'old school' in such matters, but he couldn't understand why someone who held the highest office in the land didn't 'show a bit of respect' for voters by finding a decent barber and learning to comb his hair properly. But this evening he was willing to put such prejudices aside and listen to what he expected would be an important speech with far-reaching consequences.

The tone of the message was quickly set by phrases like 'the biggest threat this country has faced for decades' and 'the devastating impact of this invisible killer'. Some general comments followed about the impact of the virus across the world and the danger of the National Health Service being overwhelmed if nothing was done. And then came the sentence that raised Albert's blood pressure and got him out of his chair to shout his defiance at the television:

*From this evening I must give the British people a very simple instruction – you must stay at home.*

He barely listened to the rest of the broadcast. For a man who'd spent so much of his life out of doors, walking the streets as a postman and turning over the soil at his allotment, it felt like a life sentence delivered by an unjust judge to an undeniably innocent man. 'Nobody,' he insisted, addressing his words to the television, 'has the right to stop me leaving my house.' He just wouldn't do it. He was in good health for a man in his seventies. Fitter than many of the people he saw in the street who struggled to walk at half his normal pace. They could fine him if they wanted to, but he wouldn't give in.

After a ten-minute walk round the estate – he assumed that the instruction wouldn't come into force until the morning or, if it did, he'd explain to anyone who asked that this was his exercise for the day – and a cup of tea, he began to calm down a little, only for his pulse to be set racing all over again when he heard something on his bedside radio about over-seventies being asked to observe an even more strict set of rules. He turned it off and tried, without much success, to get some sleep.

But now, as he looked at his lovingly cultivated allotment and drew slow, deep breaths, the sights and sounds and smells around him began to have the soothing and healing effect that he'd felt so often in this spot when something had been troubling him. He sat quietly, enjoying the tender therapy of this little patch of earth. Slowly he relaxed and the tension in his body began to ease. He gave himself a gentle but firm telling-off for allowing himself to get into such a state. A man of his age should know better than to get so worked up.

After a few minutes, he nibbled on his sandwich and sipped his by now lukewarm tea before reaching for the newspaper lying on the work bench and scanning the front-page report of the previous evening's broadcast. As he reflected on the words he was reading, he acknowledged the logic behind the lockdown. And, of course, on closer examination it was clear that there wasn't a blanket prohibition on outdoor activity. He could leave home to pick up essential shopping or to collect a prescription from the chemist. Most important of all to him was the permission to take some form of exercise every day, even if it was limited to an hour. If he didn't dally or waste time – things he never did in any case – he could walk to the allotment in just over a quarter of an hour, and that would allow him half an hour to keep a check on things and get some jobs done before he had to head home again. And if it took him just a little longer than that, he hoped the police would be too busy doing more important things than checking up on a seventy-five-year-old man who was five minutes late returning to his house.

He rinsed his mug and washed his hands again at the standing tap. When he'd dried his hands and put the mug back in its place on the shelf, he removed his gardening shoes and eased off the dungarees that he always wore over what he called his *civvies* when he was working at the allotment. He was about to hang them back on the hook behind the door when he changed his mind. No, he'd take them home today and put them in the washing machine. There might be a crisis threatening the entire world, but he'd make sure he kept everything neat and clean and tidy. 'If things around me are in good order,' he told himself, 'I can cope with most things that life throws at me.'

He put his well-polished brogues back on his feet and laced them up carefully with a double knot as he always did. He straightened up and stood still for a moment, taking one last look around him before he locked his shed and set off for home. The anxiety he'd been feeling since the previous evening had eased sufficiently for him to order his thoughts. He was surprised at the initial anger the announcement of the lockdown had provoked in him. Something he didn't know was there had been uncovered and he wondered what else might come to the surface before this was all over. There was no denying that it was a strange time, the like of which he'd never known before. No one could say what the future would hold. But he was pretty sure that whatever else did or didn't happen, come the morning, the sun would still rise, the rain would still fall and the soil would continue to yield its crop. And he'd be back tomorrow, and the day after, and the day after that, for the sheer joy of taking part in the mystery and miracle of growth that made life possible and worthwhile.

# 3
# 1st April 2020
# April Fools' Day

The weather had been pretty much what might be expected for the time of year – cool and overcast with only passing moments of brightness when the clouds had parted just long enough to allow a brief but welcome glimpse of the sun. But in every other respect, things were very different from normal. And this was an April Fools' Day like none that anyone could remember. Eight days on from the imposition of lockdown, no one was in any kind of mood for the jokes and hoaxes that were typically perpetrated on unsuspecting victims. Too many people around the country and across the world were falling victim to something far more deadly than a harmless prank or a well-executed stunt. The government had just reported the largest daily increase in the number of deaths in Britain since the start of the epidemic. On the previous day, 563 people had died from Covid-19, bringing the total number of fatalities to date to 2,352. Unlike the weather, these figures offered not even a chink of light in the prevailing gloom. Few could remember a time when the streets were as quiet and the atmosphere across Manchester was so sombre.

Albert Stridemore was not immune to the apprehension that had taken hold of his neighbours. Since returning home from his allotment at teatime, he'd been sitting quietly in his front room trying to make sense of the strange time he was now living in. A week ago, when the lockdown had first been imposed, there had been a wave of near patriotic optimism – what the newspapers were predictably and lazily calling 'the Dunkirk spirit'. A sense that the people of the United Kingdom could pull together and see off this virus with the same kind of bulldog determination and collective resolve that had launched an armada of small commercial vessels to rescue its beleaguered troops from the shores of France in 1940.

But the steadily mounting toll of daily deaths and the disturbing images of hard-pressed doctors and nurses clad head to foot in protective clothing quickly dispelled such easy optimism. It didn't take long for the truth to sink in. This was not, as some had suggested at first, a mild variation of flu that would be little more than a minor inconvenience. This was a deadly virus, an invisible enemy about which little was known and against which there would be no quick victory. And the cost, it was now becoming apparent, would be considerable in terms of both lives and livelihoods.

It raised questions for which Albert could find no ready answers. He'd long loved the beauty and trusted the healing power of the natural world. If people would only spend more time with nature, he would say to anyone willing to listen, they'd be happier and healthier. Get out and walk in the countryside, take deep breaths of good fresh air, get your hands dirty in the soil, sow some seeds and grow some vegetables. It's good for whatever ails you and it's more effective than all the pills you can swallow. It was a philosophy and a way of life that had sustained him for the past fifty years. But now he was forced to acknowledge that this potentially deadly virus that was bringing the world to a standstill and stealing the lives of vulnerable people – particularly, it seemed, those in his own age group – was just as much a part of the natural order as the grass and the trees around him.

People frequently used words like *malignant* when they talked about it. The problem with that kind of language, Albert reasoned, was that it implied some kind of consciousness in nature, some kind of evil intent. But the virus was just like the plants that flourished in the soil of his allotment. Its sole purpose was to grow and to multiply itself. And our bodies just happened to be the best environment for that process – that *natural* process – to take place. Whether Covid-19 was just the latest unforeseen twist in the ongoing vagaries of life forms that are constantly evolving or part of the mysterious plan of a distant deity, as some were suggesting, he considered himself unqualified to speculate.

He was happy to leave the complexities of natural selection to the evolutionary biologists, insisting whenever the subject had come up during a tea break in the sorting office that working out that kind of stuff was 'above the pay grade' of a humble postman. 'I get paid to deliver mail,' he would say with a shake of the head as he walked away from any debate about evolution. 'It's not my job to work out where it's all come from or how it got here.' He would leave others to speculate on the long processes that had produced the diversity of flora and fauna that fill the world today. He was content to focus his attention on the wonders he saw before him here and now and to devote his efforts to producing a crop of vegetables each year of which he could be proud.

Questions about the role of a deity in all this, however, were of a very different order for Albert. His problems on that score went back many years and he'd long ago closed the door on any conjecture related to religious belief. Whether a divine being existed or not, he was no longer sure. But he did know one thing. Even if there was a God, he seemed to be neither kindly disposed towards, nor even remotely interested in, people like him. So the matter was not worthy of his time or interest. He'd reached that conclusion through bitter experience on this very day exactly fifty-two years ago.

For years afterwards, the memory of April Fools' Day in 1968 was never far from his thoughts. He would manage to suppress it by keeping himself occupied during his working hours. But at night, after the evening meal was cleared away and his son was asleep in his bedroom, the recollection of that day would break through the barriers he'd tried to erect and come flooding back into his consciousness. Despite the early rise his job demanded, it would often keep him awake until well past midnight. But it was when the date on the calendar showed 1st April each year that the memory was at its most intense. As raw and painful as an open wound.

The banter in the sorting office was never malicious and the pranks played on one another by postmen about to set off on their rounds were never intentionally hurtful. For Albert, however, it all felt as insensitive and inappropriate as a third-rate comedian telling a succession of off-colour jokes at a close friend's funeral. Though his colleagues didn't know it, he *was* an April Fool. The *ultimate* April Fool! And the remembrance of that day could suddenly overwhelm him like molten lava pouring from an erupting volcano and covering him with a burning shame at his credulous and unquestioning naivety. The passing of time had never fully healed the hurts he carried, but it had at least numbed them to a degree that allowed him to get on with his life.

On this evening, however, as this most unusual of April Fools' Days drew to a close, he became aware of something stirring deep within him and forcing its way to the surface. It took him some moments to work out what it was that was niggling at him. And when he did, he attempted to ignore it. But the feeling simply would not leave him. He wanted – no, not wanted, he *needed* – to rehearse again the events of the day half a century ago that had changed his life for ever. Why he needed to do such a thing, he wasn't at all sure. For years he had done everything he could to stifle the memory. So why go through it all now? The closest he could come to an explanation for how he was feeling was that maybe there was something he could learn by looking back at it all from the vantage point of fifty years of life. If he'd managed to survive the anguish of that time, then there was a hope that he could emerge from the jeopardy and frustration of these days, if not unscathed, then at least able to get on with things. Or perhaps it was just that he could take some reassurance in his conviction that nothing that lay ahead of him could ever be as bad as what he'd gone through then.

He turned off the light, pulled a chair over to the open window, and sat breathing the cool night air. And then, for the first time in many years, he gave himself full permission to go through the events of April Fools' Day 1968 step by step.

The first thing that was imprinted on his mind was how the weather had changed so abruptly on that day on the north-east coast of England. The last week of March had been sunny and unseasonably warm with record temperatures in some parts of England, but by 1st April there was a decided chill in the air. He could remember thinking as he'd got out of bed that morning how crazy and unpredictable the climate in this country was. You could go from the heat of summer to what felt like the depth of winter in less than twenty-four hours. But for Albert, life was good, life was dependable, and life was in total contrast to the fickleness of the British weather. The future was assured. He and Maureen had known each other since childhood and there was only a month between their birthdays. They'd gone out on their first date when they were fifteen, but only after Maureen's parents had given their only daughter and her youthful suitor a ten-minute lecture on the dangers of what was euphemistically called back then 'going too far'. Such a major transgression, it was made clear, would not only lead to unwanted though unspecified consequences, but would also bring shame on the Watson family who had been at the heart of the life of Bornaby Evangelical Church for three generations.

Albert's respect for the Watsons ensured that he listened attentively to their warnings. They'd taken a protective interest in him ever since his maternal grandmother, with whom he'd lived since his parents had separated acrimoniously when he was just a baby, had brought him to church as a five-year-old. She was of the generation who believed that even if they themselves felt no need to attend a place of worship, all young people should receive a good dose of religious instruction so that 'they could make up their own minds' when they were old enough.

And the child had indeed quickly made up his own mind. Bornaby Evangelical Church was a good place to be. There were adults who genuinely seemed to care about him, there were young people of his own age with whom he got on well, and there was a full youth and children's programme that ensured his formative years were filled with character-shaping and relationship-building activities. It was the most natural thing in the world for him to make a faith commitment and become a member of the church when he was in his mid-teens.

And then there was Maureen. The annoying ten-year-old with pigtails and glasses who always wanted to hang around with him, despite his efforts to escape her attentions, suddenly became the girl he couldn't take his eyes off when he reached puberty and the strange but fascinating differences between the sexes started to make a whole lot more sense.

Albert Stridemore and Maureen Watson had heeded the counsel of their elders on the right way to conduct a courtship, and their marriage, six years after that first date, had been for him the beginning of a voyage of discovery into the joys of living together in holy matrimony. The birth of their son, Jeffrey, eighteen months later was seen by Maureen's family and by the wider church membership as just one more sign of God's blessing on their growing congregation. And the arrival of a personable and gifted new pastor, Ryan Rogers, with his wife and two young children the year after the Stridemores' wedding had brought a fresh impetus to the life of the church. There was a prevailing sense that this was the beginning of a new season of spiritual and numerical growth and an opportunity to impact the surrounding community for good. In fact, so much was happening at the church and so many new and innovative outreach programmes were being launched that additional full-time staff had to be recruited.

With Albert's full approval, Maureen had recently decided not to return to her teaching post in a local school, but to accept the pastor's invitation to become the youth and children's worker at the church. It had meant a considerable drop in salary for her, but they had both agreed that with what her husband earned from his one-man painting and decorating business, they would still be able to live comfortably despite the reduction in their joint income.

Only a few months into this new working arrangement, Albert found himself growing a little concerned at the demands on his wife's time and energy. It certainly meant long days. Each morning on their way to work they had to get their baby to Maureen's mother who'd agreed to provide childcare. And each evening Maureen was supposed to collect him by four o'clock. Frequently she didn't arrive at her parents' house until an hour later and often she'd be out again by seven in the evening at some youth event at church. But she was finding such fulfilment in her work that he put his concerns to the back of his mind. He was happy to support her in her ministry and grateful to be able to spend time at home with Jeffrey.

That morning, at Maureen's request, he was dropping Jeffrey at his grandparents' on his way to work to allow his wife an extra half-hour at home before she had to set off. She and Ryan – unlike his predecessor who'd been much more formal, the new pastor was keen for everyone to call him by his first name – had to travel out of town to meet a potential donor who was impressed by what he'd heard of the youth work at Bornaby Evangelical Church. Just as he always did before setting off for work, he kissed his wife. She remained standing in the doorway watching him settle Jeffrey safely into the car, and he couldn't help but notice the wistful expression on her face. He guessed that she was missing spending the days with her son and he made a mental note to talk to her when he got home in the evening about how they could readjust things to give her a bit more time at home.

The drive to his in-laws' house took less than ten minutes and his mother-in-law wouldn't allow him to set off again until she'd given him some of her home-baking from the evening before to augment his lunch. He could remember word for word their brief conversation as she had handed him the slice of apple pie wrapped neatly in greaseproof paper.

'You're a good man, Albert,' she said. There was a warmth in her voice that made him feel appreciated. 'Our Maureen made the right choice when she married you. You're our favourite son-in-law.'

'Well, I am the only one,' he responded. 'So there's not exactly a lot of competition. But I'll take it as a compliment anyway.'

He was decorating the living room of one of the church members that day, an elderly widow who was grateful to have someone in the house she could chat to and who insisted on providing him with a cooked meal at midday, despite his efforts to explain that he had both his packed lunch and his mother-in-law's apple pie with him. By four o'clock in the afternoon, feeling bloated from eating more than he needed and weary from trying to keep his focus on the job in hand while politely answering endless questions, he decided to finish early and arrive home before Maureen. It would mean he could pick up Jeffrey an hour earlier and he'd get the dinner ready, even though the last thing he wanted to do was to eat another full meal. It was a job he seemed to be doing more frequently these days as his wife was often tired, and sometimes even a little irritable, by the time she came through the door. But he really didn't mind. It would give her the opportunity to unwind and maybe there'd be a chance to have some meaningful conversation before bedtime.

When it got to half past seven and Maureen still hadn't come home, Albert was growing uneasy. She'd been late before, but never this late. Had something happened? Had she been in an accident? Or maybe, he thought a little more hopefully, she'd called in to see her folks and they'd lost track of the time. He called his in-laws but she wasn't there and they hadn't heard from her. Now he was really worried. He called the church office but, as he'd guessed, there was no one answering the phone. The only thing he could think of was to call the pastor's home number. Immediately he heard Tracey Rogers' voice at the other end of the phone, he could tell that she was worried too. She knew that her husband and Maureen had agreed to meet with someone he hoped would support the project they were planning to launch with underprivileged teenagers in the town. But who this benefactor was or where he lived she'd no idea. They were both silent for a moment. He would never forget that silence. It wasn't that neither of them knew what to say. The truth was that they were both afraid to speak, afraid of putting into words something they'd refused even to think.

Albert spoke first. 'Tell you what,' he said, trying to sound casual and hoping she couldn't hear the tremor in his voice, 'they're probably stuck in some meeting somewhere or broken down. But let's give it another half-hour and I'll ring the police. Just to make sure they haven't been in an accident.'

Tracey Rogers readily agreed with his suggestion. But the tone of her voice made it clear that she was no more convinced by his rationale than he was.

At half past eight, just as Albert was about to contact the local police, the phone rang. He let it ring three or four times before he answered it, trying to slow his breathing that had suddenly quickened. His thoughts were racing.

Would it be the reassuring call he was hoping for or the message of bad news that he was fearing? He uttered a nervous hello and waited for the person on the other end of the line to speak. To his relief, it was Maureen.

'Thank God you're alright,' he said. 'What's happened? Where are you?'

For the second time that evening there was a silence on the line. This time it was Maureen who broke it. She spoke very slowly and deliberately.

'Albert, I'm not telling you where I am. It's better you don't know that for the time being. But you need to know that I'm not coming home. I'm with Ryan. We want to be together. I'll get in touch later when we've sorted out where we're going to live. But I just wanted you to know that I'm alright.'

He could hear what she was saying clearly enough, but he couldn't take in what the words actually meant.

'What d'you mean, you're with Ryan?' he stuttered. 'Of course you're coming home. You're not making sense.'

He could feel a panic rising in his chest that threatened to push the air from his lungs. He was finding it difficult to breathe.

'I'm sorry. I don't want to hurt you. And I'm going to miss Jeffrey terribly.' The composure with which she'd begun the conversation was deserting her and she was starting to cry. 'But that's the price I'll have to pay. Ryan and I love each other. We've known it for months and we've tried to fight it. But it's not something that's going to go away. We both know we've got to be together whatever the cost.'

Now *he* was crying. Crying and begging his wife to come home. They could work this out. Make a fresh start. He'd take a hard look at himself, see where he was at fault, and try to make their marriage better. Surely she could understand what this would do to him and to her son. To her parents. To Ryan's wife and kids. To the church. Surely Ryan of all people could see that. The man was a church leader, for goodness' sake.

But his tearful pleading was all to no avail. There was no changing her mind. She was not coming home. Ryan had made a similar call to his wife, she explained, and they wouldn't be making any further contact until they'd found somewhere to live.

Somehow Albert had just about managed to hold himself together. But when she told him she was going to hang up, he lost all control of himself. He'd never liked swearing, not even as a teenager. It had always seemed to him either unpleasant or pointless. But now he erupted in a torrent of cursing. Words that he'd never used in his life before poured out of his mouth. The force of his anger took him by surprise, but he was powerless to stop it. By the time it began to subside, he realised he'd been shouting into the phone with no one on the other end of the line for the last couple of minutes. He dropped to his knees and buried his face in his hands, sobbing in despair and utter exhaustion.

Only gradually did he become aware that there was someone else in the house who was crying. Jeffrey had been woken by the sound of his father's angry shouting. Albert forced himself to get up from the floor and climb the stairs. He took the child in his arms and rocked him until he fell asleep again. Then he walked back downstairs and called Maureen's parents to tell them what had happened.

The days that followed were a blur in Albert's memory. Mostly it was his emotions he could recall rather than specific events. His shock at his wife leaving him for another man with no warning. His anger that the man in question was a church leader, admired and respected by everyone, including himself. His embarrassment as the news quickly filtered out to the congregation and gradually spread through the town. His worry about bringing up his child without a mother's care and attention.

And, overriding all these feelings, the all-pervading sense of what a fool he'd been. With the benefit of hindsight he could identify all kinds of signals he should have picked up. The amount of time she'd been spending at work. The vague answers she would give when he asked what she'd been doing when she came home late. The irritation she often displayed when she felt he'd made a mistake about something. The way her eyes lit up whenever they were in the company of Ryan Rogers. At the time he'd failed to notice them, or tried to ignore them, or come up with what he thought were plausible explanations, persuading himself they were normal behaviours and that he was just being a jealous husband. If only he'd been smarter, if he'd been more of a man, if he'd been a proper husband... he'd have tackled his wife about his concerns, spoken to Ryan about how his increasingly close relationship with Maureen was beginning to look and put a stop to it before it had gone too far. If... if... if... But he'd done none of those things. He'd been a fool. An utter fool.

People in the church were shocked and angry at the disappearance of their pastor with a married member of the congregation, and they were, without exception, kind and understanding towards Albert, the man they felt had been so badly wronged. Maureen's parents stood solidly behind him. They could find no excuse for their daughter's actions and they were adamant that no blame could be laid at the door of their son-in-law who had been, in their opinion, an exemplary husband and father.

Albert was grateful for their support. But it made little difference to how he felt. He'd been a fool not to see what was going on. He'd been a fool to give his heart so completely to a woman who could transfer her affections to someone else as quickly and easily. He'd been a fool to put Ryan Rogers on a pedestal, only to discover that all the stuff he'd been preaching to his flock about integrity and loyalty meant absolutely nothing to him. And, most of all, he'd been a fool to allow himself to believe that there was a God who knew him personally and who had some kind of overarching plan for him. Life had to go on. He had to raise his son, earn a living, try to do something useful with his time on earth. But he would never allow himself to be such a fool again.

Six months after his wife had deserted him for another man, Albert Stridemore sold his furniture, returned the keys of his rented house, said goodbye to his tearful in-laws, got into his car with his son and took the main road out of Bornaby for the last time. He vowed he would never return. Not to the town, not to the church and not to the

44

faith he'd held since his youth. He was starting life over again and he'd begin with a clean sheet. He'd decided to go to Manchester because he thought he could be anonymous in a large city, because he'd read somewhere that they were looking for postmen, and because he knew he never wanted to live in a small town or work in someone else's house again.

The first eighteen months, when they'd lived in a depressing bedsit in an even more depressing part of the city, were not easy and he was sometimes tempted to question if he'd made the right decision. But to his surprise, and for reasons he couldn't fully figure out, his name was moved up the order of people waiting for council accommodation and he was allocated a house in the Irmingshawe estate.

His divorce was finalised in 1971 and for a few years after that Maureen had demanded regular access to her son. Those were painful encounters, when the feelings he'd had for her would well up in him again. For days afterwards, he would sink into a depression that left him drained of all energy. But in 1975 she and Ryan moved to Canada. At first, she sent cards and gifts of money for Jeffrey each year on his birthday, but after a few years all correspondence stopped and he didn't hear from her again.

The Watsons continued to visit their grandson at regular intervals until ill health made travel difficult. When they died within a few months of each other in 1982, Albert grieved the loss of two good people who had never failed to treat him with respect and kindness. Their deaths, however, allowed him to close the door completely on his past life in Bornaby. He was free to stride untrammelled into his future.

And now, at nine o'clock on 1st April 2020, he realised that this was the first time he'd been able to recall that April Fools' Day more than half a century ago without experiencing all over again the pain of the events that had dealt such a blow to his confidence and self-respect. Time, he reflected with a wry smile, was indeed the great healer, even if its restorative processes could take fifty years. Or maybe, it occurred to him, it was the stillness of these lockdown days that had provided the physical and emotional resting place in which such discoveries could be made. He fell asleep wondering how long this time might last and what else there might be for him to discover before the noise and bustle of what passed for normal life flooded back in and filled the space from which it had drained away only a few days before.

# 4
# 12th April 2020
# Easter Sunday

Mr Patel was grateful that the government had recognised the importance of shops like his to the life of their community and designated them as essential businesses that needed to be kept open. Before lockdown, the more affluent car-owning residents of the Irmingshawe estate would normally do their weekly shopping at one of the supermarkets a mile or so away on the other side of the park. But for those of more limited means for whom the luxury of possessing their own transport was not even a dream, Patel's General Store was a lifeline. It was where they got their morning paper, bought their groceries, caught up with the local gossip and often returned two or three times in a day for anything they'd forgotten on their earlier visits.

And on this sunny Easter morning the genial proprietor was in good spirits as he turned around the sign hanging on the door to show that the shop was now open. The lockdown was proving to be good for business. His regular customers came in just as they'd always done, knowing they'd be greeted by name and welcomed like old friends. And even those people from the neighbourhood who hadn't shopped with him for years had begun to return. Nervous at the sight of the crowded aisles and busy checkouts at the supermarkets, where social distancing was well-nigh impossible, they'd decided that their local convenience store was not only closer to home, but also a safer bet if they wanted to stay clear of the virus. The prices might be a penny or two dearer, but they could find most of what they needed, including those items that had suddenly become more valuable than anyone had hitherto realised. Toilet rolls, magazines, paracetamol, puzzle books, flavoured gin – Binu Patel could produce them all from his stockroom at the back of the shop with a wink and a smile. He even managed to keep an adequate supply of bags of flour when his larger competitors on the other side of the park had only empty shelves.

Two minutes after the shop opened, the buzzer sounded as his first customer of the day entered. He leaned across the counter and was about to shake hands with the man who'd just walked through the door until he remembered the instructions to everyone about social distancing and quickly withdrew his outstretched hand. But his welcome was no less warm and sincere despite the lack of physical contact.

'Albert Stridemore, my dear friend, how are you this morning? I am thinking that you are coping well with this strange time. It is taking more than a nasty virus to keep you locked up at home and away from your allotment.'

Albert returned his greeting and assured him that his assessment of the situation was entirely accurate. He'd follow the rules like a good citizen, but even the might of the British government couldn't keep him away from his allotment.

The two men had known each other for many years, having arrived on the Irmingshawe estate at around the same time. A mutual respect had developed when they'd served together on the residents' association and had blossomed into a genuine friendship after the death of Binu's wife in 2010. Albert would often pop into the shop first thing in the morning or last thing at night. There was always something he needed that provided him with an excuse, but the real reason for his visits was just to savour again the pleasure of a conversation, however brief, with his old friend. He always left with a smile on his face and the world was always a better place after he'd listened to Binu Patel. The soft rhythms of his Indian accent that easily shifted the stress to a different syllable and made you hear the word in a completely new way; the sound of the vowels that came from the back of his mouth and seemed to slow everything down for a moment; the way he used the continuous present tense and made you feel you were floating along on a stream of consciousness rather than just being given some information. It was just good to hear. And always, everything he said came from a thoughtful mind and carried a quiet good sense. Albert had long suspected that Binu's mastery of English was such that he could have spoken without a trace of his accent had he cared to do so. But he was clever enough to know that it simply added to the charm and gravitas of whatever he happened to be talking about. And Binu himself had once hinted to him that it was one way of reminding his son, Pranav, of his humble roots.

'I tell him not be embarrassed about how I speak. Being a consultant might make him a big shot in that London hospital,' he'd said to Albert with a twinkle in his eye. 'But, if his father and mother hadn't been willing to work all the hours God sends in a corner shop, he'd never have had such a good education.'

Albert picked up a couple of items and dropped them in the basket he'd collected at the door. He knew his friend liked his customers to do that rather than just grabbing things from the shelves and carrying them in their arms to the counter. It was all part of the good order and high standards he was anxious to maintain.

'I'm guessing you're here for your morning paper,' Binu said, picking a copy of *The Telegraph* from the pile of newspapers behind him and putting it beside Albert's basket on the counter.

'Yes, please. And I'll take this pint of milk and a packet of digestives. I should have time for a quick cup of tea when I get to the allotment before I start getting on with what needs to be done.'

Binu raised his eyebrows questioningly as he rang up Albert's purchases and passed him his change.

'Now I am thinking this is a big change from your normal routine. Straight to the allotment, eh? Isn't Easter Sunday the one Sunday of the year when you go to church?'

Albert was about to remind him why he wasn't making his annual visit today, but before he could reply, Binu realised his mistake.

'But, of course, you cannot be going to church today. The lockdown means they're all locked up.' The juxtaposition of those two phrases made Binu laugh. 'Locked up because of the lockdown! Goodness me, what a strange language English is. And what a strange man you are, Albert Stridemore, with a strange religion that means you only go to your temple once a year.'

This was a conversation they'd had several times over the years and Albert had never succeeded in explaining his annual church visit to Binu. In truth, he'd never really succeeded in explaining it to himself.

'I know,' he responded with a shake of his head. 'It's a bit of a mystery to me too. It's such a long time since I attended church regularly. I guess that my allotment has become my church.'

He thought for a moment while Binu stood observing him from behind the counter. Albert knew from experience that this wise and kindly old Hindu always enjoyed watching him struggle to express himself. And he knew, too, that Binu was willing to wait, without uttering a single syllable, until eventually he put his thoughts into words. He tried to resist the gentle pressure of Binu's gaze and say nothing more on the subject. But almost against his will, he heard himself speaking again.

'D'you know, I was thinking the other day when I was admiring the rows of vegetables that are coming through right now, that sitting still and watching things grow gives me the same kind of feeling I used to have when I went up

51

to receive communion. Back in the days when I went to church regularly. You know what I mean... I'm looking at beans and potatoes on the allotment. Or I'm tasting bread and wine at the front of the church. They're just ordinary things. But something's happening deep inside me.'

Binu put his hands together, as if in prayer, holding them in front of his lips, still waiting and still smiling benignly. Albert had seen that posture before and it always made him feel that the truth was being inexorably drawn out of him.

'I bury hard little seeds in the ground or in a pot of compost and then I watch and wait until something rises through the soil. Something green and bursting with life. Year after year it always amazes me. And I think that's why I still go on Easter Sunday. It might be just one day a year, but it's the one day I can be fairly sure what the service will be about – dying and rising again. And when it is, it feels like... Well, it feels like, though I couldn't call myself a believer any more, I might just be holding on to some kind of truth...'

The conversation might have gone on for much longer, as their discussions often did, had not the security buzzer sounded as the door of the shop opened. Albert moved to the side, remembering the instruction to leave two metres distance between him and whoever was about to step through the door. The newly arrived customer was a bright and attractive woman, about five feet six in height, with naturally wavy hair that was greying at the temples but otherwise still retained much of its ash-brown colouring. He guessed she must be in her late sixties, but her casual knitted hoody, smart peach-coloured chinos and stylish leather sneakers sent out the unmistakable message that this was not a woman who was about to settle for becoming a sweet little old lady any time soon. He couldn't recollect having seen her before, but Binu Patel recognised her immediately and seemed to know her well.

'Mrs Finch. Good morning. I am hoping you are well today. I am delighted to see you are still intending to do your shopping in my humble establishment.'

'And I'm delighted to be here, Mr Patel,' the newcomer replied. 'When I was using the big impersonal supermarket on the other side of the park before I knew your shop was here, nobody ever spoke to me or welcomed me like you do. So I'm more than happy to give you my custom.'

Binu Patel nodded modestly and thanked her for her kind comments. As she filled her basket, he quietly explained to Albert that Mrs Finch, a widow, had moved up from London the year before. She now lived in one of the privately owned houses that looked on to the park further up Irmingshawe Road and she'd been a regular customer for the past few months. Albert was more than a little surprised by this information. He'd often delivered mail to the large residences just 500 yards along the road in his days as a postman. They were separated from the council estate only by a narrow lane, but in all the time he'd lived there, he'd never known any of the occupants from these more affluent dwellings to come on to the 'Shawe. He remembered an article in the local paper some years before that had suggested the two communities were kept apart by an *apartheid* that was based not on differences of skin colour but on discrepancies in income levels. It was clear from the way in which Mrs Finch interacted with the shopkeeper as she paid for her groceries that she felt quite at home in a place that would have been out of bounds for many of her immediate neighbours.

Albert was about to offer a polite 'G'morning' and set off for his allotment when a question from Mrs Finch stopped him in his tracks.

'By the way, Mr Patel, do you know a Mr Albert Stridemore? I need to talk to him.'

'You are wanting to talk to Albert Stridemore?' Binu laughed. 'Well, it is your lucky day. I am looking at him right now. He is standing the regulation two metres away from you, like the solid British citizen he is.'

Mrs Finch seemed delighted at her good fortune and she wasted no time in explaining to Albert just why she was so anxious to make his acquaintance.

'Mr Stridemore, I've got to know a number of the ladies in the 'Shawe from meeting them here in Mr Patel's shop. A group of them invited me to have a cup of tea with them last month before we got hit by this virus thing.'

Albert, who was by now impatient to get off to his allotment, couldn't think what this had to do with him. The irritation must have shown on his face, because Mrs Finch immediately answered the question that was in his mind.

'And I know you're probably wondering what on earth a ladies' tea party has to do with you. So, let me tell you. There are a number of families on the 'Shawe on very low incomes who are really struggling at the moment. And the chances are that things might well get worse over the next little while. So we didn't only drink tea and eat cake that afternoon. We decided to set up a food bank in the church hall. Mr Patel's agreed to put a box here in the shop where people can leave donations. We've already got a decent supply of tinned and packet goods.'

She set her shopping bag on the floor and flashed a disarming smile at Albert. There was nothing insincere or contrived in her action. But he couldn't help thinking that she knew exactly the impact it would have on him. He was aware of Binu watching the encounter with a look of amused interest and he guessed that his friend had been subjected to the same charm offensive when he'd been persuaded to support the project.

Mrs Finch looked at him appealingly before continuing with what she had to say.

'Your name's come up several times while we've been trying to work out exactly what we need to do. From everything I've heard, Mr Stridemore, you're a very accomplished vegetable grower. You and your allotment are the stuff of legend around the 'Shawe. Now, here's the thing…'

She was speaking so softly that he was having a job to hear her properly. For a moment, he almost forgot all about social distancing. He was about to take a step nearer when he stopped himself from breaching the guidelines. Out of the blue, he had a flashback to his days in primary school. Miss Brown, the formidable headmistress, used to employ that same technique of lowering her voice until it was barely audible, just to make sure every pupil was paying proper attention. Albert found himself listening as intently as he'd done seventy years before.

'It appears that many of those families on low incomes that we want to help don't have terribly good diets. You know – lots of processed foods, ready-made dinners, takeaway meals – that kind of thing. We'd like to help them discover the taste and goodness of fresh vegetables...'

'Say no more. You can count on me,' he interrupted, delighted that he could respond positively to her appeal and then be on his way. 'I'm happy to let you have some stuff from the allotment. There's always way more than I can eat. And I always end up giving away most of what I grow to my neighbours anyway.'

But Mrs Finch, though clearly grateful for his readiness to help, hadn't finished yet.

'Well, thank you. I've heard about how generous you are with your produce every year. And the other women were sure you'd be willing to do that. But we want to ask you if you'd consider doing a bit more.'

He shifted a little uncomfortably, unsure of what was coming next, sensing that the woman in front of him wasn't likely to take no for an answer. Out of the corner of his eye, he could see that Binu was still watching him closely. He could tell from the look on his face that he was thoroughly enjoying the scene playing out before him. For his part, Albert felt like the nervous five-year-old schoolboy who'd been summoned to the headmistress's office.

'It's easy enough to put fresh vegetables and some basic cooking instructions in the bags when they come to the food bank,' Mrs Finch continued. 'But what if, rather than just settling for that, we could actually teach them how to grow their own? We've been thinking that this lockdown period, when everybody will have a lot more time on their hands at home, would be a great chance to make a start. Every house in the estate has a garden, even if some are neglected. We think it could work. And the opinion of the group is that there's nobody more qualified to do that than you. So, what do you think? Are you up for it, Mr Stridemore?'

'Well, yes, that sounds like a great idea. And, of course, I'd be willing to help. But... I mean... at any other time I could take half a dozen folk up to the allotment with me. I could spend half an hour with them in their gardens. But you can't do that in this lockdown...'

Albert wasn't completely sure whether he was really wondering how they could solve the problems or if he was just hoping to wriggle out of getting involved in a scheme that was clearly well intended but that he feared would be next to impossible in practice. Whatever the truth, Mrs Finch had more than sufficient answers to his questions to block any escape route he might have been contemplating. She and the other women had thought about all that. It would be easy enough to put together some handouts – illustrated step-by-step instructions in plain English and even a couple of other languages that would show people what to do. In fact, they'd already managed to raise a few pounds to cover the cost of printing those guidelines.

But better still, she explained with yet another smile that left him in no doubt he was being well and truly press-ganged, in case he hadn't noticed, we now live in the age of the internet. Apart from some of the oldest residents, she was pretty sure that almost everyone had a smartphone and more than half of the households on the estate had some access to a basic computer. For those who didn't – well, she was about to work on some of her well-to-do neighbours who, she was certain, would have upgraded in the last year. They were likely to have their discarded but still serviceable laptops in their attics which she was sure she could persuade them to let her have. That would allow them to use social media, set up a Facebook page, link people on Zoom calls. That kind of thing. There really was no limit, she insisted, to what could be done these days with a little thought and planning.

Albert never did make it to the allotment that day. His conversation with Mrs Finch continued for another ten minutes – still maintaining the regulation two metres distance between them – on the pavement outside Patel's General Store after they left the shop. He was impressed with the title they'd come up with for the project: GGOSH: *Giving and Growing on the 'Shawe.* That, she said, would give it a strong local identity and would be easy for everyone to remember. By the time they parted, he couldn't have been more committed to the idea if he'd signed a binding contract in the presence of two witnesses. In fact, it did occur to him that had she had pen and paper handy and, had two unsuspecting passers-by with arms long enough to stretch two metres happened along at just the right moment, Mrs Finch might well have insisted on obtaining his signature on such a legal document, just to make doubly sure that he wouldn't change his mind after they'd parted.

A quick glance at his watch was enough to tell him that there wasn't time to get to his allotment and back, never mind to get any work done. He'd used up his precious sixty minutes of freedom talking to Binu Patel about burying seeds in the ground, and to a woman he'd never met before about enlisting in a venture he'd have regarded as impossible when he'd left home an hour before to pick up a pint of milk and a packet of digestive biscuits.

# 5
# 23rd April 2020
# New Skills and Old Questions

The Irmingshawe estate had been completed in 1955 as part of the post-war building programme intended to provide decent, affordable council housing for Manchester's citizens as the economy slowly picked up after the inertia of the Second World War. In contrast with the crowded tenements in which many of them had previously lived, each house had a patch of ground at the front, big enough for a small lawn, and a larger stretch of land at the back in which it was hoped residents would continue with the war-time practice of growing their own vegetables. For the first few years, gardening remained a favoured activity and working men could often be heard discussing their horticultural successes and failures over a pint in the George and Dragon. But, as television began to offer a less strenuous alternative to back-breaking sessions of digging and planting and as supermarkets increasingly provided inexpensive fruit and vegetables ready for the table, 'growing your own' became less popular and many gardens were consequently neglected.

Number 77 Park Avenue sat halfway along the street that ran right through the centre of the 'Shawe and came to an end at the junction with the main road that marked the boundary between the estate and Irmingshawe Park. The front door of the house was immaculately painted in a bright 'post office red' in celebration of the forty years the occupant had spent in the employment of the Royal Mail. It demonstrated a level of workmanship that was matched by the quality of the interior decoration. Wallpaper had been perfectly hung and woodwork painstakingly prepared and finished to a professional standard. The man who lived here was not only a retired postman for whom walking briskly in all kinds of weather was second nature. He'd also mastered the skills of interior decorating in his younger days. And though he'd followed that profession for only a relatively short time, he'd never forgotten the tricks of the trade.

But what set number 77 apart from many of the properties around it was not so much its smart front door as its garden – an exquisitely manicured lawn at the front and a series of splendidly colourful flowerbeds that skirted the side of the house and filled every available space at the back. Albert Stridemore's talents as a gardener were not limited to growing rows of potatoes and swedes and carrots and beans in his allotment. When admiring passers-by complimented him on his work and asked him how he found the time and energy to maintain a spectacular garden at home while managing to cultivate his prize-winning vegetables a mile away on the other side of the park, he had a ready answer. Echoing words he'd first memorised as a boy when his grandmother had dropped him off at Sunday school in the hope that it would 'do him some good', he would smile thoughtfully and reply, 'Well, men and women cannot live by bread alone.' Then he'd go on to amplify his biblical allusion by explaining that if the vitamins and minerals in vegetables provided the nourishment necessary for a healthy body, it was the beauty and fragrance of flowers that offered much of the sustenance needed for our souls. There's no point in having a well-fed belly, he'd opine, if you have a half-starved heart. He wasn't always sure that his audience knew exactly what he meant by that. But he was content in the knowledge that just seeing and smelling the flowers would have done them good.

This afternoon, however, though the sun was shining and the sky was blue, Albert was neither tending the flowers in his garden nor cultivating the vegetables in his allotment. It would have been a surprise for his neighbours, none of whom would ever have thought of him as a 'silver surfer', had they been able to see him sitting at the kitchen table in front of his recently acquired laptop computer. After his conversation with Mrs Finch he'd hurried home and scribbled down what she'd said before the words and phrases she'd used would slip from his mind. He'd only the vaguest idea of what was meant by words like *internet, online, social media, Facebook* and *Zoom calls*. But he wasn't going to admit that to someone like Mrs Finch. So he'd made two phone calls. The first was to Patel's General Store. His friend, he was sure, understood all about this stuff. Binu relied on his computer for everything to do with his business. And he'd often teased Albert, telling him that he really needed to 'get into the twenty-first century'.

Then, when Binu had provided him with a basic vocabulary to use so he didn't sound like a complete fool, he'd made a second phone call, to Irmingshawe Computer Supplies, asking them to deliver a laptop as soon as possible. He'd also ordered an instruction manual, explaining that he was new to this kind of thing and he needed one that avoided fancy jargon and would tell him what to do in plain English. The helpful young man on the other end of the phone told him he knew exactly what he needed. He'd got one for his grandad just a few weeks before and he'd been able to understand it without too much bother.

The same helpful young man had personally delivered his order a week ago, since when Albert had spent every afternoon and well into each evening working to develop his previously non-existent IT skills. He made painfully slow progress at first. It felt like he was having to learn a whole new language spoken by some alien race from a far distant planet. But, with constant reference to his instruction manual and repeated calls to his ever-patient shopkeeper friend, he was beginning to get the hang of it. And even before his computer had arrived, Binu had somehow managed to persuade the telephone company that it was their civic duty to pull out all the stops and install broadband for the elderly gentleman at 77 Park Avenue. Mr Stridemore, he'd informed them, was 'a pillar of the community' and urgently needed to get online for his role in a project that was crucial for the health and well-

63

being of the residents of the 'Shawe during the current Covid-19 crisis.

Albert continued to hone his skills through the afternoon and well into the evening until, as had happened more than once since he'd begun his IT education, a sudden pang of hunger reminded him that he hadn't eaten since lunchtime. He was normally fastidious in his eating habits, believing that regular, well-prepared meals and a wholesome diet were essential to a healthy and active life. But tonight, too tired and hungry to do anything else, he was happy to settle for a couple of poached eggs on toast which he ate from a tray on his lap while watching one of the news channels on television.

He hadn't realised it until the presenter pointed it out, but it was exactly one month to the day since the beginning of the lockdown. Day after day he'd followed the news as the death toll continued to rise ever more steeply. He'd experienced the sense of shock felt by so many at those terrible statistics. It was an emotion that had been heightened by the news that the Prime Minister himself had been struck down by the virus, becoming so ill that he'd had to spend time in intensive care. His first thought, apart from his basic sympathy for a fellow human being in distress, was that if even those in such powerful positions could not protect themselves from the disease, what chance did ordinary folk like the residents of the 'Shawe have of avoiding its reach.

But, as a former employee of the Crown with a profound respect for Queen and country, the moment that had made the greatest impact on him had been the sovereign's message to the nation from Windsor Castle earlier in the month. He thought she'd got the balance just right in emphasising the gravity of the crisis, acknowledging the important contribution of those who were working every hour to bring us back to normality, and in offering hope for the future. He'd been so impressed that he'd written down her closing words on a slip of paper that he'd attached to his refrigerator where he could look at them every day:

*We should take comfort that while we may have more still to endure, better days will return: we will be with our friends again; we will be with our families again; we will meet again.*

It was a sentence tucked away in the earlier part of her speech, however, a sentence that he hadn't written down, that fixed itself in his mind. Try as he might, he couldn't get it out of his thoughts:

*Once again, many will feel a painful sense of separation from their loved ones.*

Albert was, of course, well used to living alone. And he was comfortable with his own company. Whole days would sometimes pass on his allotment without him saying more than two or three words to anyone else. He was grateful for conversations with a good friend like Binu Patel, but he craved and valued the times of solitude and the opportunity to be alone with his thoughts and memories. The fact was, apart from not being able to spend as long at his allotment, life in lockdown was not really that different from how he'd lived for years.

But, however often he reminded himself of that, the phrase wouldn't leave him alone: *a painful sense of separation from their loved ones*. The longer it went on, the more he was forced to acknowledge why it kept coming back to him. The painful sense of separation he was feeling now wasn't a result of the present restrictions. Not for the first time, he noticed the disconcerting way in which things he'd kept buried for years were being uncovered. He could no longer suppress it. The ache in his heart wasn't the unwelcome consequence of a national lockdown. It was the unhappy outcome of a family break-up.

At the time, it had been fairly easy to explain his son's sudden departure in the summer of 1988 to anyone who asked. Jeffrey had an opportunity of a job in Canada that was too good to refuse. It meant dropping out of university, but he'd only just turned twenty-one, so there would be plenty of time to pick up his studies later. And it was true – as far as it went. But it was far from the whole truth. Remembering his own troubled childhood and mindful of the fact that he was a single father raising his son without the help of a wife, Albert had been scrupulously conscientious in carrying out his responsibilities as a parent. He did his best to ensure that the boy grew up in a home where love and discipline were present in equal measure. And it had worked. Father and son got on well together and Jeffrey had always shone at school. His teachers predicted a bright future for the lad.

The problems had started when he'd turned sixteen and his hitherto safe and secure home life began to feel suffocating. Back in the early sixties, Albert had found a place of sanctuary in the structured youth activities of Bornaby Evangelical Church where he'd fitted in easily. A quarter of a century later, he found it difficult to understand the natural desire of a teenage boy to assert himself. There was nothing particularly extreme in Jeffrey's rebellion. His school work didn't suffer and he was never in trouble with the police. But there were occasional late nights and frequent loud music from his bedroom and a number of friends that his father didn't approve of.

Had there been a wife and a mother in the family to act as an intermediary, the difficulties might have been resolved without any lasting damage being done to their relationship. But, with no one to take on that role, the gulf between them became ever wider and the atmosphere ever more strained. The more the son tried to kick over the traces, the more his father sought to assert his control over him. He wasn't being unreasonable, he told himself. The boy had the opportunity to do something with his life. Opportunities that he'd never had. All he wanted was for him to make the best of himself.

Jeffrey saw things from a very different perspective. By the time he left for university in Birmingham they were barely on speaking terms. He did come home for the summer at the end of his first full year and they managed to negotiate a truce. For a week or two the ceasefire seemed to be holding and they both began to wonder if they could salvage their relationship. But a furious row had broken out when Albert had discovered Jeffrey smoking cannabis in his bedroom late one evening. Jeffrey had protested that it was no big deal, just something that everyone did at university. It was no different, he argued, from having pint of beer or a glass of wine, and arguably less harmful. But for Albert a line had been crossed. The thought of illegal drugs being used in his house was something he couldn't countenance. He ordered his son to leave that night, forbidding him to return until he'd come to his senses.

A month later, Jeffrey called his father to tell him that he was dropping out of university and going with a friend to Canada where they hoped to find work. He'd phone again, he promised, once he'd found a place to live.

Albert had never been able to explain to himself why he'd ended the call without telling the boy to come back, telling him that he loved him, telling him that he'd overreacted in forcing him to leave home – telling him anything that might have changed his mind and saved their relationship. He hadn't even said goodbye to his son. He'd just listened without uttering a word until Jeffrey had finished speaking. Then he'd said, 'OK, if that's what you've decided to do, you're old enough to take responsibility for your actions.' Then he'd abruptly ended the call. He knew he'd done the wrong thing as soon as he put the phone down. He'd apologise when he got the call from Canada and put things right. But the weeks and months went past and the call from Canada never came.

For the first few years he'd hoped that it would all work out in the end. He imagined a reunion just like in the parable of the prodigal son. He'd be looking out of the window one day and he'd see Jeffrey coming up Park Avenue with a rucksack on his back. He wouldn't wait for him to reach the door. He'd run out to greet him in his slippers, they'd both say sorry and embrace, and they'd walk into the house arm in arm. They'd have an impromptu party. Invite the neighbours in to share their celebration.

But Jeffrey never did return. And when that hope died, Albert made a series of enquiries. He contacted the Canadian Embassy in London, but they could find no trace of anyone by the name of Jeffrey Stridemore who fitted the profile. A colleague at the sorting office mentioned that he had relatives in Toronto who belonged to a club for British ex-pats and that it might be worth getting in touch with them. That, too, yielded nothing. He wrote letters to people he'd known who'd emigrated to Canada on the off-chance that they'd met his son. But all his efforts were to no avail. And in the end, he resigned himself to the fact that Jeffrey was lost to him.

From time to time, he would talk about it to Binu who was always sympathetic and willing to listen. There were occasions, however, when those conversations left him feeling even more of a failure as a parent and made his sense of loss all the more acute. Binu had three adult children and five grandchildren. One daughter was at university in Leeds and another was married with children and living elsewhere in the city. And, of course, there was his son, Dr Pranav Patel, of whom he was justifiably proud. Unlike Jeffrey, Pranav had never given his parents a moment's concern. When he was twelve, he'd won a scholarship to an independent school, from where he'd gone on to study medicine at the University of Edinburgh, graduating with outstanding grades and following up his degree with a number of postgraduate qualifications. Now he was, as Binu often expressed it with a beaming smile, 'a big man in a big hospital'. Albert's affection for his friend was such that he never allowed his irritation to show. But in his heart, he couldn't help thinking how unfair life had been to him and how lucky Binu had been.

Albert had learned how to bear pain, both physical and emotional. He sometimes got home around five o'clock in the evening, having toiled in the allotment from early morning, weary to the bone and aching in every limb from his exertions. That kind of soreness could always be eased by taking a couple of ibuprofen, steeping himself in a tub of warm water for half an hour and getting a good night's sleep. And fifty-two years after his wife had left him, the memory of her departure could still suddenly return, sharp as ever, and stinging like an open wound that refused to heal. Moments like that could not be dealt with by swallowing a pill or taking a bath. But he knew that if he just kept going and stayed busy, the throbbing intensity would ease and allow him to get on with life.

The pain he was feeling right now, however, was different. The hurt had not been done *to* him. It had been done *by* him. Done to his only son. How had he managed to live with it for so long? And nothing could be done to heal the hurt or to put things right after all these years.

Despite his disappointment with some of the younger members of the royal family, Albert remained a staunch monarchist with an unshakeable respect for the Crown. He wouldn't have dreamed of remaining seated during the playing of the national anthem, and he listened attentively to the Queen's speech every Christmas Day.

But he wished he'd never heard her speak those words – *'many will feel a painful sense of separation from their loved ones'* – in her address to the nation. And he wished even more that he'd never put the phone down on a boy who was about to leave for Canada and who was his only real *loved one* in all the world.

He would have sat there until it was time for him to go to bed, lost in melancholy thought, had he not been startled by the sounds of cheering, hand-clapping and saucepan-banging coming from outside his window. For a second or two he couldn't think what on earth was giving rise to such a commotion. And then he remembered. It was eight o'clock and it was Thursday. He hurried to his door and added his voice and applause to the general hubbub.

For some more sedate neighbourhoods, raising a ruckus once a week might initially have felt like an undignified way of registering their appreciation for the hard-pressed staff of the National Health Service and others working on the front line. For the residents of the 'Shawe, however, it had seemed the most natural thing in the world. Making a noise was what you did when you wanted to celebrate or say thanks. And that evening it had the immediate effect of lifting Albert's spirits in a way that nothing else could have done.

When the din subsided, he went back into his house feeling a little better than when he'd stepped out just a few minutes before. Yes, there were things he'd done wrong and that he'd always regret. And there were people he'd loved and lost and whom he'd always miss. But, in the middle of a pandemic that threatened life itself, goodness and gratitude were still all around.

# 6
# 1st May 2020
# Fame and Misfortune

The last time the 'Shawe estate had featured on the local evening news had been back in the autumn of 2015 when complaints from some older residents about antisocial behaviour by groups of young people had led to what a local newspaper called 'an increased police presence in the area'. The article had not elaborated on this description, probably because explaining that the 'increased police presence' had consisted only of two slightly bored police officers driving around the streets for half an hour on two consecutive evenings would have immediately killed the interest of their readers.

Determined not to be outdone by their competitors in the print media, a television news team had arrived on the scene a day or two later on a cold and rainy Thursday evening intending to interview three or four irate old ladies on their doorsteps and expecting to film hordes of teenagers rampaging up and down Park Avenue. In the event, the old ladies, who were settling down with their cups of tea in front of their televisions to watch their favourite soaps, refused to answer their doors. And the teenagers, who'd sensibly decided that a wet evening was no time to be rampaging anywhere, were playing computer games in their bedrooms.

After scouring the estate in the pouring rain for something that would provide them with a story, the reporter had managed to find two very wet-looking, though unfortunately for his purposes, not very articulate thirteen-year-olds. The boys, who presumably weren't lucky enough to have a games console in their bedroom, had decided to compensate for this lack of home entertainment by letting off a few fireworks. Their amateur pyrotechnics display was duly captured on film. Such was the effect of the rain on their damp firecrackers, however, that even the loudest bang was of insufficient volume to disturb a stray cat that happened to be wandering aimlessly past at just the right moment. The result was that the two-minute item on the local news the following evening was, in more senses than one, something of a damp squib. The appearance of the soggy feline, one local wit remarked, was the most exciting moment of the report. Bob Morris, the producer, had taken such umbrage at what he considered a waste of time and resources that he'd vowed that nothing short of mass murder would tempt him to send anyone to that part of Manchester again.

But one good news story that had featured in the media for weeks had persuaded Bob that it was time to relent and despatch some of his people back to the 'Shawe. The story of Tom Moore, a ninety-nine-year-old retired military officer from Bedfordshire had been on every national news bulletin for days. Captain Tom, as he'd become known, had set out early in April to walk ten laps round his garden each day until he'd raised £1,000 for the NHS in sponsorship from friends and neighbours. His exploits had caught the imagination of the wider public and by his 100th birthday on the last day of the month, he'd raised the staggering total of more than £30 million.

'We need a story like that,' the head of news broadcasts had told Bob, waving a copy of the morning paper in front of him. 'We're having to show depressing figures daily of elderly people in care homes here in the north-west falling victim to Covid-19. Older viewers are going to become so depressed by it all that they'll just switch off. Find me some *good* news. Something that'll give them a bit of hope. I want a story about older people. Not just about how they're self-isolating and avoiding the virus. Something about how they're actively doing stuff in the community. And I want to get something on tonight's programme.'

As he hurried back along the corridor, Bob remembered an email that he'd received a week or so earlier from a Mrs Finch who lived opposite the park on Irmingshawe Road. He was always getting messages like that and he'd probably have deleted this one right away had something else not distracted him. It certainly hadn't seemed worth following up at the time. But he was desperate now. And though he couldn't remember exactly what it had said, he did remember something about older people getting involved in something called GGOSH that they hoped would benefit the entire community.

As soon as he got to his desk, he brought Mrs Finch's email up on the screen. Now that he looked at it properly, he could see that it was intelligently written, with well-constructed sentences and proper paragraphs. And, to his relief, there wasn't one word in the block capitals so beloved by viewers whose primary purpose in communicating was to get five minutes of fame and their face on the telly. He hesitated for a moment when he realised that the project she was describing was based in the 'Shawe. But he hadn't anything else and they were launching the thing in less than an hour at two o'clock. There wasn't any time to be wasted. He summoned his chief reporter to his office and handed her a printout of the email.

'Jacqui, get yourself out to the 'Shawe estate with a cameraman and see if you can make a decent feature out of this. It seems to be a food bank with a difference. It's being set up by two or three older folk. And Mrs Finch, whoever she is, sounds like she's got all her marbles. The boss is on the warpath, demanding a feel-good story for this evening's edition of the programme. Don't let me down. Or I might be out of a job and needing the help of a food bank myself by the end of this week.'

Jacqui Aldred would have liked to have taken a moment to glance through the email before setting off on her assignment. But Bob Morris was already ushering her out, demanding to know what she was waiting for and instructing her to call the writer of the email and let her know they'd be covering the launch of her project.

Half an hour later Jacqui and her cameraman arrived in the 'Shawe to be greeted by the sun breaking through the clouds and a small group of people standing on the grass in front of St George's Church in the middle of the estate, all of them dutifully adhering to the instructions to observe the regulation two-metre distance between them. She quickly identified Penny Finch who was obviously in charge of the proceedings and who introduced her companions: Mrs Nancy Williams, the local councillor; the four other women who made up the steering committee of GGOSH; the Reverend Olivia Smithers who'd readily agreed to the request that the project should be based in the church hall; and her partners in crime, as she described them, Mr Binu Patel and Mr Albert Stridemore, without whose support the thing would never have got off the ground. She also pointed towards three teenagers standing on the edge of the group, two boys and a girl, explaining to Jacqui Aldred that without waiting to be asked, they'd volunteered to deliver food parcels to elderly folk and others whose health conditions meant that they were unable to leave their homes. And the taller of the two boys, she said pointedly, would be filming the launch on his phone so that it would be available online for everyone to see.

'So you see,' she concluded, aiming a gentle rebuke at the impressed reporter, 'even if you'd ignored my email we'd still have a record of the event.'

All this time, Albert Stridemore looked on, equally impressed by the manner in which Mrs Finch had got things organised. What he admired most was that she'd done it without it feeling like a one-woman show. He'd never seen anyone with such a knack for getting people involved while also succeeding in deflecting all the credit from herself on to them. The ten-minute launch that followed was, he thought, a perfect illustration of how she went about things. While Mrs Finch stood back and kept a watchful eye on the proceedings, Councillor Williams set the ball rolling, welcoming everyone and praising the community spirit of the people who lived on the 'Shawe; one of the committee members read a brief prepared speech explaining what *Giving and Growing on the 'Shawe* was all about; the vicar offered a brief blessing; and Binu cut the ribbon that was stretched across the door of the church hall and declared the project well and truly launched. Albert, who hated the thought of any kind of public speaking, was relieved that he hadn't been asked to take part in the simple opening ceremony. As he'd already discovered, a request from Mrs Finch would have been difficult to refuse.

Every home on the estate had been leafleted with news of the venture during the week and people were already gathering to avail themselves of the help being offered. And Albert had willingly accepted the responsibility of organising the twenty or so eager clients who were first on the scene into an orderly queue, making sure that they kept a safe distance from each other. Being a man with a passion for good order, he'd volunteered for the task, knowing it would be well within his comfort zone and presumably well clear of anybody carrying a camera or holding a microphone. He chatted with each new arrival as he assigned them a place in the line, completely unaware of what was happening just behind him. Hearing someone call his name, he turned round to find Mrs Finch with Jacqui Aldred and her cameraman.

'I need to introduce you to Mr Stridemore,' Mrs Finch was saying. 'His role in the project adds a great deal of value to what we want to do. Not just to offer help, but hopefully to empower folk to help themselves. You really should take a moment to interview him.'

Albert shook his head and raised his hand in protest at the suggestion. But before he could get the word 'No' out of his mouth, there was a microphone on the end of a two-metre-long pole pointing in his direction. And the young woman holding the pole had already put her first question to him.

'So, Mr Stridemore, tell me about your role in *Giving and Growing on the 'Shawe.'*

Jacqui Aldred fixed her gaze on him and Mrs Finch nodded encouragingly from the side. It took him what felt like a very long time before he succeeded in stringing some words together.

'Well… I've always been a keen gardener. I spend nearly all day over at my allotment.' He quickly remembered to correct himself. 'Well… I mean, I did until this virus thing happened and everything changed. I still get there most days, even if it's only an hour or so. Anyhow, Mrs Finch thought that maybe I could be of some help to other people living on the 'Shawe.'

His interviewer smiled encouragingly and Mrs Finch made a kind of mime of clapping her hands without actually making any sound.

'So I'll be showing folk how to grow their own vegetables. Help them eat a bit more healthily and save some money at the same time…'

By the time the interview had ended, Albert had answered several more questions and talked for more than two minutes. He'd been so nervous that he couldn't remember exactly what he'd said. He just hoped it hadn't been anything silly or embarrassing. Jacqui Aldred seemed pleased enough, and she gave him a thumbs-up as she and her cameraman got back into their car.

'That was great,' she called out enthusiastically. 'You came across really well, Mr Stridemore. You've got the knack of sounding like you're telling the truth. And, Mrs Finch, I think you've got a great thing going here. Worth us following up on. I'd like to come back in a couple of months and do a feature on how it's all progressing.'

At home that evening, though he'd have been ashamed to admit it to anyone else, Albert had cleared up after his dinner in good time to make sure he was sitting in front of his television at precisely half past six, ready to watch the local news right from the opening credits. Twenty minutes into the programme, having resigned himself to the fact that they must have decided not to show the item about GGOSH, he was just about to switch to another channel when the presenter announced that tonight they'd be ending the programme with a good news story. And then, to his delight, images from the afternoon's launch filled the screen, including a fairly lengthy clip of *his* interview. In his entire life to that moment, Albert had never made as much as a fleeting appearance on television, not even as part of a crowd at some large event. He felt a rush of pride at what he was watching. It was good to be part of something that would help his neighbours and show the Irmingshawe estate in a good light to others in the city.

He'd just turned off the television and was heading into the kitchen to make a pot of tea when the phone rang. It was Binu. No doubt he too had been watching the programme.

'Hello, Binu,' Albert interrupted his old friend good-humouredly as soon as he realised who was calling. 'I'm guessing you've been watching the news. And now that I'm a TV star you want me to do a personal appearance at Patel's General Store. Bring in some more custom.'

But Binu hadn't been watching the programme. He'd called for quite a different reason. And it was immediately clear from his voice that he wasn't in any mood to laugh at Albert's attempt to be funny.

'I am needing to talk with you, Albert Stridemore.'

'Is something wrong, my friend? You sound really worried.'

'Yes, something is wrong and I am very worried. It's my son, Pranav. His wife has just called to let me know that he has caught the Covid-19 virus.'

'Oh, I'm sorry, Binu.' Albert wanted to be reassuring as well as sympathetic. 'But he's young and healthy. They reckon that most younger people get over it very quickly without any long-lasting problems. And he's a doctor. He'll be alright, I'm sure.'

'Well, as you are saying, he is young. And I am hoping he will be well soon. But being a doctor is the reason he has caught the virus. He's been caring for coronavirus patients since it all flared up in London. Now he's been ill for ten days and his wife is telling me that he is getting worse. He asked her not to tell me when he first became unwell because he was not wanting to worry me. But things have become so serious that she is feeling she needs to let me know. If his condition is not improving by tomorrow morning, they are going to move him into intensive care. It is sounding very bad to me.'

Albert's first thought was to put the phone down and walk round and sit with him in his flat above the shop for an hour or so. Let him talk things out. He'd done that occasionally over the years when Binu had something on his mind, especially since his wife had died. But, of course, the lockdown regulations wouldn't allow him to do that. All he could do was listen sympathetically and try to offer some comfort and support. He'd been doing that for quarter of an hour when Binu had to end the call.

'Thank you for listening, my friend. I must stop. The girl who is looking after the shop goes home at seven thirty, so I need to get down there and attend to the customers. It will keep me occupied for the next few hours. I'm not sure exactly how a man who is going to church only one day a year is saying his prayers. But, however you are doing it, I will be grateful if you will add your Christian prayers to my Hindu mantras.'

For the rest of that evening, Albert struggled to sort out everything that was going through his mind. Of course, his overriding emotion was one of sympathy and genuine concern for a man who'd come to have such an important place in his life. He'd had numerous acquaintances and he generally got on well with people. But his friendship with Binu Patel was the only close relationship he'd formed in all the years since his marriage had broken down. They were from such different parts of the world, raised in such different cultures and nurtured in such different faiths. Most people would have assumed that they would have had little in common. Yet, thrown together by seemingly random circumstances, their shared humanity and their need for companionship had forged a bond between them that neither of them could ever imagine would be broken as long as they lived. And his feelings of sympathy were sharpened with pangs of regret. Regret for the times when he'd looked at Binu and thought how lucky he was with his long marriage and his happy family. The times when he'd lamented the unfairness of life that had left him on his own, divorced from his wife and separated from his son. The times when he'd foolishly allowed himself to forget that we all live in a dangerous world where anything can go wrong for any one of us at any moment.

Then there was the plea for him to add his 'Christian prayers', as Binu had put it, to all the mantras being chanted and all the entreaties being offered up for the recovery of Pranav Patel. He'd trouble with both words Binu had used. For a start, he was pretty sure that he no longer qualified to be called a Christian. Yes, he'd tried to live a decent life and not hurt anyone else, though he didn't think he'd ever quite managed to love his neighbour as much as he loved himself. And he certainly wouldn't describe himself as an atheist. It was difficult for him to understand how anyone who'd watched the dry little seeds he'd buried in the soil emerge as green living plants could ever be as adamant as that. He still thought – maybe *hoped* would be more honest – that there had to be *Something* or *Someone* that gave meaning to life. And he'd never forgotten the stories from the Gospels that he'd known since childhood. But if he was ever asked to put his hand on the Bible and say that he was a believer – *a Christian* – he'd draw the line at that. You don't want to make claims like that if you're less than 100 per cent sure!

Prayer was another tricky word. He never bowed his head, closed his eyes and clasped his hands like he once did. Not since the day he'd got into the car and taken the road out of Bornaby all those years ago. Admittedly, from time to time he'd mutter things like 'please God' when he was anxious about something or when he saw images of people suffering on the news. And he did sometimes find himself asking for patience or strength or wisdom, though who he was petitioning or whether it constituted what could be described as prayer, he wasn't at all sure.

But Binu was a dear friend. And Pranav was undeniably seriously ill and in need of all the help he could get. So for five minutes he tried to pray. He simply said over and over again, 'I'm asking for Pranav Patel to recover.' It wasn't much compared to the mantras and chants that Binu and his fellow Hindus would be presenting to Brahman. But it was the best a man who couldn't honestly call himself a believer could do. And, if there was Someone listening who cared and had the power to do something, he hoped he would intervene to heal Pranav Patel. He went to the kitchen, made the tea he'd been intending to make when Binu called, and thought to himself how life in a time of pandemic uncovered longings that had lain dormant for a long time.

# 7
# 8th May 2020
# Strange Times and Changed Days

Walking at his customary brisk pace, it seldom took Albert Stridemore longer than sixteen and a half minutes to lock up his shed, walk through Irmingshawe Park, cross the road and arrive back on the 'Shawe. This afternoon, however, he was surprised to discover when he glanced at his watch that it had taken him more than half an hour from leaving his allotment to reaching his front door.

This rare disruption to his normally precise timing had resulted from an uncharacteristic delay. Having come through the gates of the park, he'd paused, intending only to wait for a gap in the traffic that would allow him to cross safely. But what was meant to be a momentary suspension of his journey had somehow lengthened into a fifteen-minute stop as he sat down on one of the boulders that marked the perimeter of the park, and gazed across the road at the housing estate where he'd lived for these last fifty years. He wasn't exactly sure why he'd stayed sitting on an uncomfortable lump of stone for so long. Perhaps it was just the exertions of the morning and the warmth of the afternoon sunshine that had caused him to feel the need to rest. More probably, it was the fact that this was a day for reminiscing. The entire country had been encouraged to stand still and look back to the day seventy-five years earlier when the nation had breathed a collective sigh of relief at the surrender of Nazi Germany and the end of the Second World War in Europe.

Whatever had prompted his unexpected train of thought, Albert had yielded to the sudden urge to break his homeward journey. He sat with his hands on his knees, gazed across at the 'Shawe, and reflected on the strange days and changed times in which he was living. At first glance, the estate didn't look all that much different from when he had first arrived. The same long rows of houses, their walls covered in the same grey cement rendering, sitting unpretentiously on the same unremarkable streets. But anyone who'd lived there as long as he had knew that things *were* different.

The changes had come slowly at first but, as the years passed, they became ever more apparent. In many of the houses, those grey rendered walls now had gleaming satellite dishes attached that brought large-screen, high-definition images and cinema-quality surround sound into front rooms where once black and white pictures had sufficed for home entertainment. In others, the front gardens, sacrosanct to the enlightened planners who'd been inspired by the garden city movement of the first half of the twentieth century, had been paved over or tarmacked to provide additional off-road parking spaces for one and sometimes two cars.

The process of transformation had been accelerated by the right-to-buy policies of the Thatcher years when those occupants who could afford to do so had purchased their houses from the local authority with 100 per cent mortgages at prices substantially below market value. And these new homeowners had often chosen to flaunt their new status by building extensions and making modifications to their property that would trumpet their liberation from having to rely on the council for repairs and renovations.

Albert had watched these changes with a detached amusement. He was satisfied with his lot and had no ambition either to spend his money on the latest and largest home entertainment systems or to become his own landlord. He did, however, observe with genuine interest the deeper changes that were happening to what had been an almost totally white, working-class neighbourhood. Not content just to settle for the right to buy their council property, those residents of the 'Shawe with ambitions to be even more upwardly mobile had gradually upped sticks and migrated to the numerous private estates that had mushroomed around the city in the last twenty or thirty years. And, as they had moved out, their places had been taken by people from a variety of ethnic backgrounds. In the past, Binu Patel and his family had been the sole representatives not only of the Indian subcontinent but also of almost the entire non-white peoples of the world. Now, as well as second- and third-generation immigrants from the Caribbean and various African countries, there was a small Bangladeshi community and three Syrian families who'd been granted asylum.

Back in the eighties, Albert recalled, there had been some initial teething troubles, and tensions still flared up from time to time. He knew from his period as chair of the residents' association that there were a few diehards on the estate with distinctly racist tendencies who were unlikely ever to alter their thinking. And there were some in the older generation for whom change of any kind was difficult. But progress had been made. He'd worked hard during his two terms of office to make sure that all residents, irrespective of colour and ethnicity, were treated equally in housing matters and were fairly represented on the membership of the group.

Now, as he re-emerged from number 77 Park Avenue at four o'clock, having washed and changed into a suit and tie, he allowed himself to feel just a little proud of the hard work that he and others had done over the years to bring the community together. Tonight the 'Shawe would be celebrating the seventy-fifth anniversary of VE Day. Of course, all their original plans had been scrapped. The coronavirus had put paid to all that. There would be no brass band concert in Irmingshawe Park, no talent competition for the kids, no late-night dancing to the hits of the 1940s at the community centre. But, undismayed by the strictures of social distancing, his neighbours had strung red, white and blue bunting and set up their tables and chairs. They'd keep within their own family groups in their front gardens and they'd observe the stipulated two-metre distance between them. But they would party into the night to commemorate a victory in a war that had ended before most of them were born. It would have been a cause for celebration at any time. But at *this* time, when the country was facing an unseen enemy that had already taken more than 20,000 lives, it was good to have a reminder from 1945 of what could be achieved when people pulled together.

It was almost ten o'clock when Albert carried his folding table and chair back into the house, leaving his more youthful neighbours to linger a little longer over the festivities. He sat down with a cup of tea and watched the images on the television news of similar celebrations up and down the country. Once again, the oddness of these days struck him. While so many people were fighting for their lives in hospitals and care homes, thousands were sitting in front of their houses, raising their glasses and singing patriotic songs. It wasn't easy to reconcile such opposites in his mind.

As powerful as the impulse to remember the past had been, he surmised, people had been even more grateful for a day that would stand out from every other day in the past few months. He'd always been organised, always knew what he should be doing on any particular day. Mondays he did the bulk of his shopping for the week, Wednesdays and Saturdays he left the allotment at two o'clock so that he could spend time in the garden at home, Fridays he did his housework in the afternoon, and Sundays he'd often take the tram into the centre of Manchester and go to the cinema or visit one of the city's museums. But now he frequently had to remind himself which day of the week it was. Last Thursday, when was picking up some things from Patel's General Store, he'd asked Binu why he was still trying to sell him Wednesday's newspaper, only to be told it *was*

Wednesday and that he was twenty-four hours ahead of the rest of the world.

And there was something even more odd. A weird kind of contradiction that intruded itself into every interaction and seemed to set everyone on edge. Albert had overheard it again and again, even at two metres' distance or in snatches of conversation when he was striding through the park. At one moment two people would be talking about the monotony of it all, how every day was the same. Each one indistinguishable from the day that preceded it and the one that followed. And, in the next moment, they'd be voicing their fear of the changes that might lie ahead, the fear that 'life will never be the same again'. It felt to him as if collectively people had unknowingly pressed the pause button at a crucial moment in some television drama in which they'd all become absorbed. Now they wanted to know what came next. But, try as they might, they couldn't find the controls to restart the video.

The whole country was stuck in a weird limbo where nothing altered from day to day, but where everyone suspected that when change did eventually come, things would not end well. Of course, there were brief interludes when a desperate optimism took over, like shafts of sunshine in an otherwise dark and stormy sky. Maybe, he thought, when this is all over, we'll take steps to protect the environment, maybe we'll value the NHS more, maybe we'll pay workers on low incomes a proper living wage, maybe we'll all be nicer and kinder people. Maybe, maybe, maybe...

Albert had always wanted to understand things, to make sense of life. His formal education had ended abruptly at fifteen. His grandmother couldn't afford for him to stay on at school, so he'd started work as a painter and decorator, the first job he could find. But he'd never been afraid of hard work and he had an eagerness to keep on learning. Throughout his adult life he'd made it a practice to read a serious newspaper, often to the derision of his workmates who couldn't see why the tabloids weren't good enough for him. He still kept up with events on the world stage, watching current affairs programmes on television and engaging in thoughtful conversations on all kinds of topics with his great friend Binu. At seventy-five, he'd reached a time in life when phrases like 'in the next twenty-five years' would cause him to smile and think wryly to himself that he probably wouldn't be around by then. But that was far from being a morbid thought. His awareness that he had a limited number of years ahead of him served only to sharpen his appetite to make the most of every day while he still had all his faculties.

He had his regrets, of course, especially over his estrangement from his son. But regret by itself was a wasted emotion. There was no point in brooding over the past. And the only conclusions he'd been able to reach about how to deal with this strange time were that it wouldn't last for ever and that it offered a unique opportunity to look and listen and learn. To discover – perhaps *uncover* would be a better word – things that he would otherwise have missed. That would be the best preparation he could make, whatever happened next and however long or short his life might be. And no one could know what tomorrow would bring.

He didn't have to wait until the morning, however, to face the unpredictability of life. The phone by his bedside rang at half past eleven, just as he was drifting off to sleep. Nobody ever called him at that time of night and it woke him with a start. He wondered if it was one of his neighbours. Maybe the street party had got out of hand. It only needed one or two people to have too much to drink. But it was Binu.

'I am sorry to be calling you so late, my friend. I was going to wait until the morning, but I am needing to speak with you.'

He guessed immediately that something was very wrong. Binu never rang at this time of night. His early rise to ensure everything was ready for opening the shop by seven-thirty meant he was always asleep by now.

'Are you alright? Is it Pranav?'

'Yes, it is. They put him on a ventilator this morning. I wasn't wanting to bother you then. It's supposed to be a day of celebration. And I hoped everything would be OK. But his wife called me a couple of hours ago. His condition has got worse very quickly. They are telling her that there is little hope of him surviving through the night.'

'I'm so sorry, Binu. What can I do to help?' But even before he'd finished the sentence, Albert knew what he would do. 'I'm coming round to your house right now. I'll be there in ten minutes.'

Binu protested that the government's current regulations wouldn't allow him to do that. It was an objection to which Albert responded with an uncharacteristically rude statement about what the government could do with its regulations. Then he put the phone down, got dressed quickly and strode out of his house.

An hour later, two police officers driving slowly through the estate, just to make sure that the celebrations were over and that everyone had retired for the night, were surprised to see two elderly gentlemen sitting on folding chairs two metres apart outside Patel's General Store. Sergeant Pickering knew the 'Shawe well. It had been part of his beat as a young constable and he immediately recognised both men. He got out of the patrol car and walked slowly towards them with a quizzical smile on his face.

'Now what on earth are you two old-timers doing out at this time of night? You should be indoors. Getting your beauty sleep. I could have you both locked up for breaking the law.' As he got nearer, however, he could see from the expressions on their faces that something was troubling them. His tone became serious. 'You haven't had your shop broken into, Mr Patel, I hope?'

'No, everything is fine in the shop. But I've had some very bad news, Sergeant Pickering.' Binu stood and walked towards the police officer as he spoke. 'I'm afraid my son, Dr Patel, is very sick in London. He has the coronavirus. I called Mr Stridemore to share the news and, being the good friend that he is, he insisted on getting out of his bed and coming round to offer me some comfort.'

At quarter past one in the morning, having listened sympathetically to Binu and seen him safely back indoors, the experienced police sergeant reached number 77 Park

Avenue. He'd walked with Albert while his colleague drove the patrol car slowly alongside them.

'Mr Patel is a lucky man to have a friend like you,' he said, as he got back into their vehicle. 'Let's hope that things might improve and that the morning brings him some better news. But, however it all turns out, he'll need your friendship.'

Albert stood for a moment, breathing in the cool night air and watching the police officers drive off. Life was an uncertain business. There was so much he didn't know and would never know. But, as he turned the key in the lock and stepped back into the house, he was sure of two things. He was grateful to have a friend and glad to be a friend. And whatever the morning would bring, those were the things that would help them get through.

# 8
## 16th May 2020
## Meetings Virtual and Real

A few weeks before, *videoconferencing* had been just another of those clumsily concocted words that irritated Albert Stridemore: one that he'd heard from time to time with no clear idea of what it meant other than that you needed a computer to indulge in it. This morning, having recently become the owner of what he'd been told was a 'decent entry-level laptop' and having invested hours getting the hang of it, he was doing exactly that. He was *videoconferencing*! Hosting his first Zoom conversation, albeit somewhat nervously. But even his anxiety about getting it right couldn't diminish his excitement watching the faces of the other four participants appear on the screen as, one after the other, they joined the meeting. Videoconferencing really did work! And it really was possible for a seventy-five-year-old to enter this strange new world of digital technology.

He cleared his throat and read the opening remarks he'd written out and placed to his right on the wooden stand that was normally used for propping up one of his cookery books when he was trying out a new recipe. He'd had one of his younger neighbours check his notes, just to make sure he'd got the jargon right. Well, the last thing he wanted was to look like an old fool who didn't know what he was doing.

'Good morning, friends. Welcome to the first online meeting of GGOSH vegetable growers. I think you've all had the email with the agenda attached. So you know that the format for the meeting is simple. Each of you will give a brief report on how you're getting on with your vegetable growing, using the screenshare facility to present any photographs you want to show, I'll answer any queries you have and we'll wind up with some general discussion. I just need to add that it'd be helpful if you could raise your hand any time you want to speak. That'll make sure we don't talk across each other and cause the sound to cut out.'

There were nods and murmurs of agreement and he could see that the others were impressed by his hard-won mastery of the medium. Not surprisingly, there were one or two hiccups as they went along, but after the first five minutes things ran fairly smoothly. There were questions about the best way to weed and the right time to water in what was turning out to be an unusually dry spring; there was enthusiastic debate on what could still be planted successfully and what would have to be left for another year; there were proudly displayed photographs of beans and onions and cucumbers and broccoli and cabbages and turnips and swedes; there were sympathetically received confessions of the inevitable failures of first-time gardeners; and there was even a round of applause when one resourceful member of the group carried his laptop into the garden to show them the tomatoes he was growing in the makeshift greenhouse he'd constructed from stuff his neighbour had left out ready to take to the recycling depot. By the end, everyone agreed that their first Zoom meeting had been a success and that it was well worth doing again.

Albert shut down his computer, sat back in his chair and breathed a sigh of relief. It had gone well for a first time. But it surprised him just how exhausting it had been. He was used to hard work. Until the lockdown had curtailed his day, he could do eight hours on his allotment and still have the energy to cook himself a proper dinner when he got home. But just one hour doing this was wearying in a way he'd never experienced before. Making sure that everyone had the chance to have their say was tiring in itself. But trying to read their expressions, listen between the lines and respond appropriately demanded a level of concentration that left him feeling completely drained. He could see that videoconferencing – he'd even started to use the word himself – was a great boon at a time like this. But he'd never before felt such a longing for a simple face-to-face conversation with someone sitting on the other side of the kitchen table. That wasn't possible right now. So he did the next best thing. He lay down on his bed and fell sound asleep.

An hour later he woke feeling not only refreshed but also hungry. He was thinking about making himself some lunch when the phone rang. Pranav Patel was still clinging fiercely to life, but for the last week Albert had been dreading the phone call from Binu with the bad news that they both knew was inevitable. This time, however, it was a woman's voice. A woman he knew! She sounded cheerful and he relaxed immediately.

'Albert Stridemore, it's Penny Finch here. Now, tell me. Are you busy this afternoon?'

He realised that although they'd met several times since their first encounter in Binu's shop on Easter Sunday morning, he'd never known Mrs Finch's first name. Their meetings had always been with Binu and the others who were involved in getting GGOSH up and running. And, though she'd quickly delegated the chairing of those meetings to one of the other women in the group, everyone still readily deferred to her obvious experience and expertise. It seemed natural to him to address her as Mrs Finch. And she'd always referred to him as Mr Stridemore.

'Well... I was going to head up to my allotment,' he replied hesitatingly. 'But everything's in pretty good order there. So, if you need my help with something, I can easily leave that until tomorrow.'

He surprised himself by his willingness to change his plans. For the last ten years, everything else had taken second place to his gardening. But, of course, he'd committed himself to help with GGOSH, so he was duty bound to be available when needed.

'Oh no,' she laughed. 'I don't need you to *do* anything. You've done more than your fair share over the last four weeks. In fact, you deserve a rest. That's really why I'm calling you. The weather seems quite settled again today and I thought you might like to come and have lunch with me in my back garden.'

Albert was not an unsociable man. He regularly sat with a group of the other growers around one of the communal picnic tables the council had set up in the middle of the allotments. He often popped into Patel's General Store at times when he knew the shop would be quiet to have a cup of tea and a chat with Binu. And occasionally he called into the George and Dragon on a Friday evening for a half-pint of bitter in the company of some of his neighbours. But he hadn't been invited out for a meal in years and he was momentarily nonplussed as to how he should respond to an invitation from a woman he felt he barely knew.

'Well, I wouldn't want to put you to a lot of trouble. And won't we be breaking the lockdown rules if I come to your house?'

As soon as the words had left his mouth, he knew he'd said the wrong thing. And that set him worrying in case he'd offended someone who was trying to be kind to him. He was trying desperately to think of what to say next. Penny Finch, however, was neither offended nor put off by his hesitant reply.

'It's no trouble at all. And, no, we won't be breaching the guidelines, if I'm understanding them properly. They changed a couple of days ago. Provided you don't come into the house and we stay in the garden and keep to two metres between us, we should be fine. It'll be nice to chat over some food.'

He could see that she wasn't about to take no for an answer. So he thanked her for the invitation and said that he'd be glad to come for lunch.

'Good,' she replied, sounding genuinely pleased at the prospect of his company. 'I just remembered that you were doing your first Zoom meeting this morning. I know how tiring those conversations can be and I thought you could do with someone making you a nice midday meal. And you can tell me all about how it went while we eat. My house is the third one along on Irmingshawe Road after the lane. Number 5. I'll crack on with getting it ready for twelve o'clock. Don't be late.'

Now he was in a quandary. Should he wear a suit? Did he need to take a gift? And lunch sounded a bit pretentious. What if she made something really fancy that he didn't like or couldn't eat? After fifteen minutes of agonising over what he should do, he settled for the sports jacket and flannels he'd bought back in January and hadn't yet worn, picked a bunch of his best blooms from the garden, and decided that he'd eat whatever was put in front of him without question.

He arrived on the doorstep of number 5 Irmingshawe Road at precisely fifty-nine minutes past eleven and nervously rang the doorbell.

'I guessed you were the kind of man who'd turn up right on time,' Penny Finch called out as she came along the path from the back of the house and took the flowers that he held out. 'You know, I hoped you'd bring some of your flowers. These are beautiful, thank you.'

He followed her as she turned back down the path and into the well-kept garden at the back of the house.

'I like to keep things tidy,' she said, as she noticed him casting his eye over the lawn and flowerbeds. 'I'm afraid I don't have your green fingers. But take a seat. Just give me a moment to put these in water before I serve up the food.'

She took the flowers into the kitchen and Albert sat down at the table that had been set for two, complete with napkins. He tried to remember the last time he'd been a guest at an *al fresco* lunch, but without any success. He'd just begun worrying again about what he'd do if he was served anything he really couldn't eat when his hostess returned carrying a tray with a rack of warm toast and three tureens that she laid on the table. She removed the lids to reveal their contents. The first contained warm mashed avocado, the second had bright red cherry tomatoes, and the third was filled with the fluffiest scrambled egg that he'd ever seen. His fears about what might be on the menu disappeared immediately at the sight.

'Now, first of all,' she said, as she waited for him to help himself and fill his plate, 'can we agree to dispense with formalities and call each other by our first names? Are you alright with Albert and Penny? Sounds more friendly than Mr Stridemore and Mrs Finch, I think.'

Had not his hunger won out over his manners and caused him to pop a mouthful of egg in his mouth before his hostess had served herself, he would have responded with a definite yes to her suggestion. Not wishing to spray the egg in her direction, however, he had to content himself with a brisk nod of his head, an action that resulted in making them both laugh. He was already beginning to relax and enjoy the meal. And his pleasure only increased when Penny poured the tea into a china cup using a strainer.

'Oh, a proper cup of tea,' he observed admiringly. 'Teabags are fine when I'm drinking from a mug at the allotment. But it's not like loose leaf tea from a nice cup.'

And so, sitting two metres apart, drinking proper tea from delicate china cups and chatting easily under a pleasantly warm sun, the friendship of Albert Stridemore and Penny Finch began. They talked about Albert's Zoom call that morning, about the progress of GGOSH and about the changes in their lives enforced by the lockdown. And when they'd exhausted those topics and Albert was thinking that the polite thing to do would be to say thank you and leave, Penny leaned forward in her chair and pushed the conversation on a little further.

'Now, I know you've been living here a long time. But you're not a Mancunian, are you? I think I can detect from your accent that you're from the north-east originally. So, what brought you to this part of the country?'

Albert had never told anyone other than Binu about his life prior to coming to Manchester. Those who'd known him from the time he'd arrived on the 'Shawe with his eighteen-month-old son had deduced that either bereavement or the breakdown of his marriage had robbed him of his spouse. But their attempts to offer sympathy or enquire about his history had been met with a polite but resolute silence. This was the first time in many years that anyone had asked him directly about his past and his intention was to deal with the question as he'd always done before. However, either the passing of the years had brought a measure of healing he hadn't before appreciated, or the peacefulness of that moment in Penny Finch's garden had weakened his hitherto unbreachable defences. Or maybe it was the strange power that life in lockdown seemed to have to bring things unexpectedly to the surface. Perhaps it was a combination of all three. But for the next half-hour he allowed the whole story to bubble up and tumble out – being raised by his grandmother and taken to Bornaby Evangelical Church, growing up and falling in love with Maureen Watson, discovering the terrible truth of his wife's infidelity with the pastor of the church, facing the shame and embarrassment of the weeks and months that followed, taking his child and relocating to a city where no one knew him, losing contact with his son. He told his story as honestly and simply as he could.

'And that's my life's history,' he said, when he got to the end. 'It's probably a lot more than you wanted to know. I've never told it to anyone other than my friend, Binu Patel. To be honest, I'm not sure why I've burdened *you* with it. It's not as if it's all that interesting.'

'You haven't burdened me at all,' Penny replied, shaking her head. 'And it *was* interesting. People's stories usually are, in my experience. Maybe it was that loose-leaf tea that weakened your defences and loosened your tongue. But seriously, I know you a whole lot better for hearing it. And after all, I *did* ask you.'

'And I could hardly refuse after eating such delicious food and drinking such excellent tea. I suppose that's what they mean when they talk about singing for your supper. But can I ask about you? What made you move to Manchester?'

'Well, I guess fair's fair. But the tea's gone cold by now. Let me make a fresh pot and then I'll tell you my tale. And, by the way, if you need the loo before you drink another cup of tea, there's one round the side of the house. The folk who built this place back in the fifties had the good sense to include an outside toilet.'

If the promise of a second cup of tea was music to his ears, the additional information of the availability of an outside loo was equally welcome. Like the offer of a lifebelt to a drowning man. It was such a long time since he'd spent a whole afternoon in the company of a member of the opposite sex that he'd no idea of the etiquette governing how to broach the subject of his increasingly pressing need. He silently blessed the memory of the foresighted person who'd insisted on amending the plans to include a lavatory that could be accessed from the garden without entering the house.

By the time the tea was being poured, he'd made good use of the facilities and returned to his place, much more comfortable than he'd been five minutes before and ready to hear her story, however long it might take.

It didn't take long at all for Penny Finch to outline her professional life. It was, she explained, something she'd done so often in interviews that it was just like a script she'd memorised and could perform at a moment's notice. She'd been raised and educated in Manchester until she'd gone off to university in London at the age of nineteen. After graduating, she'd settled in the capital and carved out a career in education. In the mid-nineties, she'd become the head of a failing secondary school in one of the more deprived boroughs of the city, succeeding in transforming it over a decade into something of a model for similarly struggling schools. And by the start of the new millennium she'd risen to the position of director of education in the same borough, a post she'd held until retiring in 2015.

'I guess most people would consider that I've had a successful career. And I've certainly enjoyed my work. But that's not the whole picture by any means. On a personal level, things were sometimes far from easy. And, looking back, I think progressing in my job was a way of compensating for the difficulties at home.'

She looked into the middle distance and for a moment or two she seemed lost in thought. Albert wondered if she'd decided that she'd allowed herself to say more than she'd really intended. But a thoughtful smile slowly crossed her face as she began speaking again.

'Do you realise how odd this conversation is?' she asked. 'Here we are, two people in their seventies who met only a few weeks ago, keeping a safe distance between us to protect ourselves, but making ourselves vulnerable at the same time by revealing the details of our lives. Including the bits we don't normally share with anyone else.'

'Well, this strange time is doing funny things to people,' Albert observed. 'It seems to be giving us all the space and time to say things we wouldn't have said before. You're right. It is odd how being forced to keep our distance from each other has brought many of us closer together. I know I haven't talked to anybody quite like this for longer than I can remember. So, if you're happy to carry on, I'm certainly willing to hear your story.'

The story that Albert heard began with a happy childhood in an affluent suburb of Manchester. Penny

Carter was the only child of parents who doted on her and made sure that she wanted for nothing. She'd gone to an expensive private school in the city where she'd excelled both in the classroom and on the sports field, becoming head girl in her final year. Her time at university had been equally successful and she'd emerged into the world of work with an outstanding degree that assured her of employment on the teaching staff of an even more prestigious private school than the one she'd attended as a pupil. It was there that she met and fell in love with Reginald Finch, the handsome and talented head of the music department with a growing reputation as a young composer of genuine potential. In 1970 they'd been married in Reginald's home city of Dublin, and the future looked rosy for the newlyweds whose friends and family regarded them as the perfect couple.

She paused at this point, picking up her napkin and folding it neatly into a triangle, as if she needed to prepare herself before she continued.

'I've never actually read any of those romantic paperbacks you see in the newsagents,' Albert commented, as he waited for her to continue with her tale. 'But from what I gather, it sounds as if your story would be just right for one of those.'

'I guess it does,' she laughed. 'But only up to this point. I'm sure we've both learned that life doesn't always have a happy-ever-after ending.'

Penny dusted the crumbs from the table with the napkin before putting it back on the plate in front of her. She spoke more slowly now, weighing her words carefully as she picked up from where she'd left off.

'Things went just as everyone had predicted they would. Our marriage was all we'd hoped for, I was getting on well in my job, and Reginald had a number of commissions that brought in extra income and added to his burgeoning reputation as a composer. And, to make our happiness complete, after we'd been married seven years, I got pregnant with our first child.' She paused and corrected herself. 'Our only child.'

Albert regretted the flippant comment he'd made just a minute before. What he was hearing now was far from a tale of unbroken wedded bliss. The Finchs' first and only child was a little fair-haired boy. As everyone agreed that he'd definitely inherited his father's good looks, they named him Reginald. His parent's early joy at his birth slowly gave way to a niggling concern as they became ever more worried by his failure to make the progress they'd expected to see. After the first nine months he was unable to sit up on his own. At eighteen months he showed no signs of being able to walk. His movements were uncontrolled and jerky. And, as time went on, it became obvious the boy had difficulty with his speech and vision. Their worst fears were confirmed when they were given a diagnosis of cerebral palsy.

'That would have been a challenge in itself,' Penny said. 'Every parent wants their child to be healthy and well. And it became obvious as time went on that in addition to his physical disabilities, he would have significant learning difficulties. But it wasn't the end of the world. Reggie was a sweet child, a lovable kid with a real personality and a mind of his own. And with a bit of financial help from both sets of grandparents we were able to afford some additional care and support. That really helped. And he's become a lovely man. He's lived far longer than we were told to expect at the beginning. In fact, he's the main reason I moved back up here. But I'll get to that later. The real problem that we faced was that Reginald found it difficult to deal with it...'

She took hold of the napkin again. But this time it was to wipe her eyes. Albert desperately wanted to be sympathetic, but years of living alone meant he'd lost the talent for finding the right words to say to a woman with tears trickling down her face. So he sat quietly until she felt ready to speak again.

'I learned to accept what had happened. And it was always easy for me to love Reggie. I didn't have to find a reason for my son's disability. There wasn't a reason. We live in a world where accidents occur, sometimes things go wrong, some kids are born with disabilities. It's nobody's fault. It just happens. But my husband couldn't come to terms with it. He'd blame himself. Then he'd blame me. Then he'd blame the doctors who'd looked after me during my pregnancy. Then he'd blame God, even though he insisted he was an atheist. He'd have periods where he'd get back on an even keel and I'd think he'd got over it at last. But he never did. And he'd suddenly erupt into bouts of irrational anger. There were times he'd even be aggressive to me. I'd never really worn make-up until I started using it to hide the bruises on my face so people at school wouldn't find out what was going on at home. Those were difficult years.'

She paused again. The tears had gone, though there was no doubt in Albert's mind that she'd been deeply hurt by what she'd been describing. Now, however, there was a different light in her eyes, as if those tears had washed away any temptation to self-pity or to wallow in the pain of the past, leaving only a resolute wisdom that had come at great cost. There was worse still to come in her account of her earlier life, he suspected. But, looking at her across the table, he was sure that in the end this would be a story of victory rather than merely survival. Again, he resisted the urge to comment and waited for her to resume her story.

'Eventually, after we'd been married for just over twelve years, the situation became intolerable. By that time, we'd managed to get Reggie into a very good residential school. He was really happy there and we'd have him home sometimes on weekends and during the holidays. I hoped this would ease the pressure on Reginald, let him get his life back on an even keel, give us space to work at re-establishing our relationship. But things just got worse. He couldn't cope with his teaching job. Gave up composing. Wouldn't leave the house in the end. Looking back, I can see that having a child with cerebral palsy wasn't the real problem. That was just the thing that triggered my husband's depression. We'd probably deal with it better today. In some ways 1980 seems just like yesterday, but we weren't nearly as aware of mental health issues as we are now. And maybe, if I'd been less busy with work, I could have done more to make sure he got the right kind of help. But that's all ifs and buts and maybes. It's always easy with hindsight...'

She unfolded the napkin and smoothed it flat on the table. She ran her hand over it several times, as if she was drawing some comfort from the clean, soft white cotton before continuing.

'It was a wet Thursday evening – the week before Christmas. And I got home at exactly nineteen minutes past six. I remember looking at my watch before I fumbled in my bag for my key to let myself in. The house was quiet, but there was nothing unusual about that. I didn't ever bother to call out. Normally Reginald would hear me open the door if he hadn't fallen asleep in front of the television. He spent most days just sitting watching daytime television while I was out at work. But after I'd kicked off my shoes and dropped my bag on the floor, I went looking for him. He wasn't in the house and I began to get worried. He never went out anywhere…'

She picked up the napkin again and held it in front of her mouth. A minute must have passed before she put it back on the table and clasped her hands in front of her.

'I wondered about ringing the police. But I told myself it was too soon to do that. To this day I don't know why it came into my head, but I suddenly thought I should go and look in the garage. He *never* went there. He didn't drive and he definitely wasn't interested in DIY. But that's where he was. That's where I found him. I almost tripped over the stool lying on its side. He must have used it to stand on before he kicked it away. He was hanging from one of the beams. It was an awful thing to see. Our next-door neighbour was a retired police officer. I stood on his doorstep unable to get the words out to tell him what had happened, but he could see that something was wrong. I'll always be grateful to him. He took control of the situation…'

'I'm so sorry,' Albert said. He wanted to say more. Something understanding and helpful. But he knew that anything he said would be unequal to her grief. He wanted to reach across and put his hand on hers. But he didn't do that either. It would have been overfamiliar. It would have breached the social distancing guidelines. It just wouldn't have been right. So he sat still and allowed her to cry. He was shocked by what he'd heard. Shocked even more by the sight of this woman, whose competence and confidence had so impressed him, looking so vulnerable and fragile. And he was fascinated as, after a little while, he watched her dry her eyes with the napkin, crumple it into a ball and smile at him. It reminded him of those times when an unexpectedly heavy shower of rain would force him to huddle in the shelter of his shed, thinking that there would be no more gardening that day. Then, as the rain stopped, the sun would break through again and he would emerge and return to his tasks, grateful that what had seemed like an interruption was, in truth, the means by which everything was renewed and nourished and life was made possible.

'Thank you for listening, Albert. It's been good for me to talk. I haven't spoken about it in a long time. I've been needing to let it all out for a while. I coped at the time by making sure that Reggie was alright and throwing myself into my work. That's when I decided I needed to leave the comparative shelter of private education and move into the state sector where I felt I could make more of a difference. Heading up an inner-city school with kids from difficult backgrounds was hard work, but it was totally absorbing and satisfying and it stopped me thinking about myself. And it was great preparation for my next job trying to give a lead to all the schools in the borough. Work's been my salvation, as they say. And work's pretty much what I've been doing ever since then. Even after I retired, I was focused on working out the best time to make the change and finding the right house to move into. It's only since I moved back up here that I've given myself permission to slow down a little.'

She stood up and began to clear the table. She didn't appear to be embarrassed at shedding tears and it seemed to Albert that she'd completely recovered her composure.

'I'm not sure that you've slowed down all that much,' he replied, raising his eyebrows. 'You've worked hard with that group of women from the 'Shawe setting up GGOSH. But you mentioned that Reggie was the main reason you came back up to Manchester.'

'Oh yes! Reggie...' She put the tray down on the ground and sat down again. 'Well, I did a bit of research online and discovered a very good residential facility on the outskirts of Manchester that I thought would be just right for him. And it's turned out to be as good as I hoped. He likes to be independent, but his condition is such that he'll always need a fair bit of care and support. And this place is halfway between a group home and assisted living. It's perfect for him. The staff are excellent and he's made some real friends among the other residents. I was visiting him a couple of times a week until this virus hit and they thought it best to stop visits. But once the lockdown is lifted, I can go regularly again and have him home for weekends. You must meet him. I think he'd like you. He loves anything to do with plants and gardens.

Maybe you'd show him your allotment when we get out of this time.'

Albert agreed that he'd be delighted to return Penny's hospitality by welcoming mother and son to enjoy tea and digestive biscuits in the slightly less salubrious surroundings of his small but cosy shed. And, having extended that invitation, he judged it was the right time to express his gratitude and head for home. He walked past the park and crossed the lane that marked the beginning of the 'Shawe at something less than his usual brisk stride.

It had been a day of two very different meetings. Two meetings that made him think that dangerous as the coronavirus was, and inconvenient as the lockdown had been, they had brought with them some unexpected opportunities to get to know people with whom he might otherwise have considered himself to have had little in common in more normal times.

# 9
# 26th May 2020
# Grief and Anger

It was a refreshingly cool Tuesday morning and Albert Stridemore was still in a deep sleep when the phone rang at six o'clock. He'd gone to bed late, having spent much longer than he'd intended surfing the internet on Sunday evening after a full day on his allotment. When he'd finally logged out and turned off his laptop, he'd told himself that he should know better at his age than to stop up so late. He remembered ruefully how dismissive he'd been only a few months before when he'd heard someone on the radio referring to people in his age range as 'silver surfers'. Now he understood all too well just how addictive accessing the internet could become.

He sat up on the edge of the bed, pushed his feet into his slippers and hobbled stiffly into the hallway. He picked the receiver up, still struggling out of sleep and into wakefulness, with a sickening feeling in his stomach at the thought of what he might be about to hear.

'Hello, Albert.' It was, as he feared it would be, Binu's voice. 'I am sorry to be disturbing you at this time of the morning. But I am calling to tell you some very bad news. My boy, Pranav, died late last night.'

It took less than one minute for Albert to express his sympathy and tell the grief-stricken father that he was coming straight round to see him, and less than ten minutes for him to get there. Just as they'd done on that night more than two weeks before when Binu had told him of his son's worsening condition, the two men sat in front of Patel's General Store and talked. What pained Binu most was that neither he nor any family member had been with Pranav when he died. And none would be able to be present at the funeral. But he took consolation in the knowledge that a *pujari* had been present and the proper Hindu rites had been observed. The *pujari* was an old family friend who had also agreed to officiate at the cremation that would take place in the next twenty-four or forty-eight hours.

'It is a dreadful loss for you, Binu, and you will miss him terribly.' Albert desperately wanted to comfort his friend. 'But you raised your son to be a good man and you should be very proud of him. The virus has cruelly cut short his life, but he lived it well. He devoted it to caring for others.'

Binu nodded in gratitude at Albert's words. He gave a deep sigh and took his time before responding.

'You are right, my friend. He has done much good in this life. And I must accept what has happened as the outworking of *karma*. We are all part of that cycle of life and death and rebirth, always moving on.'

Albert was always uncomfortable when their conversations arrived at this place. It was impossible for him not to respect the quiet and dignified manner in which Binu faced the trials and tribulations of life. He was a *good* friend, the best friend he'd ever had. He was, by any standard, a *good* man. He and his wife had raised *good* children who had grown up to be *good* citizens who lived *good* lives. And Albert could see that Binu drew great strength and many profound and timeless truths from the religion he followed with such devotion. But he could never rid himself of the sense that there was something unutterably sad in his resigned acceptance of a process of repeated reincarnations that seemed to have no real ending. He could see that Binu knew exactly what he was thinking at this moment.

'We have been talking about these things many times before, Albert Stridemore.' Binu had that same patient half-smile that Albert had seen so often. 'And because we are such good friends we can be agreeing to disagree. Though sometimes I am thinking that in the end what you are believing and what I am believing may not be so different.'

At other times, this would have been the point in the conversation at which Albert would have protested that there was 'clear blue water' – that was the phrase he always used and that always made Binu laugh – between resurrection and reincarnation. And Binu would have pursed his lips before saying very quietly, 'I wonder, I wonder...' And Albert would have got frustrated and almost shouted, 'That's the trouble with you, Binu. You don't ever disagree with anything.' And Binu would have stroked his chin in a theatrical manner and objected, 'Well, I am not understanding how a man who is attending his church on only one day a year can have such absolute certainty about things.' And they would both have laughed and agreed that they'd have to return to the subject later.

But on this morning, in the face of the reality of the untimely death of a young man who should have lived for so many more years and in the midst of their grief at such a loss, they neither argued nor laughed. On this morning, it took all the strength of Albert and Binu to cling on to their hopes – different as they might be – that the virus that had ravaged the lungs of a much-loved son and a highly respected doctor was not the final reality. And on this morning, two men in their seventies, one a devout and practising Hindu and the other a lapsed and uncertain Christian, disregarded the rules of lockdown, got up from their seats two metres apart and, with tears running down their cheeks, embraced each other in the doorway of Patel's General Store. It was neither a temple nor a church, but for a fleeting moment on this morning, it felt to them both that they were standing on holy ground.

'Now there is work that is needing to be done,' Binu said, releasing his hold and wiping his eyes. 'I cannot be standing here crying all day. I must be ready to open the shop. People are still needing to be fed.'

The moment had passed and, remembering their civic duty to observe a proper social distance between them, they stepped back from each other. Binu went into the shop and began preparing for the arrival of his first customer and Albert went home, ate some breakfast and set off to lose himself in a day's hard toil.

The majority of the residents on the 'Shawe were grateful that this was turning out to be the sunniest and driest May month that anyone could remember. People could frequently be heard calling out to each other from across the street how the weather was making lockdown a whole lot more bearable than would have been the case had Manchester lived up to its reputation for being one of the rainiest parts of the country in which to live. But, while Albert shared their pleasure in the warmth of the sunshine, he was not nearly so pleased about the lack of rain. Dry ground would yield little harvest. So his first task on arrival at the allotment was to get down on his hands and knees, scrape away the topsoil with a trowel and push his finger as deep into the earth as it would go to check just how dry it had become.

It was a trick he'd learned long ago from an experienced allotment owner that had stood him in good stead over many years. It told him all he needed to know so that he turned on the hose for just the right amount of time. He avoided the danger of overwatering while making sure that he never allowed the ground to dry out to the point at which the plants would suffer. Not knowing when to stop watering, he'd learned, could be as bad for the health of his vegetables as not watering enough.

It made him think of his conversation with Binu earlier and of all the debates they'd had over the years on the topic of life after death. He was right to question his friend's beliefs, but he wished he'd always shown the same good judgement in recognising when to stop pursuing his argument and simply trust that truth would emerge out of honest and courteous dialogue. He concluded wryly that he'd learned more about gardening successfully than he had about arguing sensitively.

There was more than enough to be done on the allotment to keep him busy well into the afternoon. The unusually sunny weather meant that many of the jobs he would normally have left until June could be done now. He thinned out the beetroot and carrots and turnips; he planted broccoli and summer cabbage; he made sure the netting was intact where the birds would have feasted if he'd left the plants unprotected; he checked the undersides of the brassica leaves and painstakingly picked off the innocent-looking little white and yellow eggs that would have hatched into caterpillars and devoured the fruit of his labours; and, before he called it a day, he sowed some sweetcorn and imagined how good they'd taste in a few months' time. That was enough to remind him just how hungry he was. It was time to tidy up and set off for home.

He was striding through the park, still thinking about the tasty sweetcorn and feeling even more hungry when he heard someone calling his name.

'Mr Stridemore! Albert Stridemore!'

The voice coming from one of the benches beside the pitch-and-putt golf course fifty yards to his left was that of Brenda Braithwaite, a long-time resident of the 'Shawe with a well-deserved reputation not only for finding out everything that was happening on the estate, but also for devoting much of her time to relaying the news of her latest discovery in excruciating detail to anyone she could persuade to stop and listen. Not wanting to be delayed from his dinner, his first thought was to pretend he hadn't heard her and keep on walking. But Brenda, despite her advancing years and her considerably less than sylphlike figure, was already hurrying across the grass. Albert, who was too much of a gentleman to continue with his subterfuge, stopped to allow her to catch up with him. He could hear her panting for breath as she drew nearer.

Oh, Albert,' she gasped. 'It's been such a day for bad news. Do you know about Mr Patel's son?'

He confirmed that he had indeed heard about Pranav's death from the coronavirus and explained that he'd spoken with the bereaved father earlier in the day. But, having found someone she judged to be a willing listener and recovered her breath sufficiently, Brenda had more sad tidings to impart.

'And that's not even the half of it,' she said, dabbing her eyes with a handkerchief. 'We've got it right on our own doorstep.'

Albert, who'd been figuring out how to excuse himself and get home for dinner without being rude to a woman, hesitated when he heard these words.

'What do you mean, Brenda, on our own doorstep? I don't know anyone on the 'Shawe who's got the virus.'

'That's what we all thought, Albert. That's what we all thought...'

Brenda was finding it almost impossible not to allow her pleasure at telling him something he didn't already know to overcome the display of grief she felt was appropriate to what she was about to share. She wiped her eyes with her handkerchief once again and gave several loud sniffs just to make sure she could be seen to be observing the proper decorum required when reporting such sad news.

'We were wrong, Albert, we were wrong. Old Mrs Milner died last night. She's lived in the little cul-de-sac across from the church since those houses were built. She'd been in hospital for just over a week. I spoke to her older son this morning – the one who lives on the other side of the estate. He told me it was definitely the virus. Said she had terrible trouble breathing before she passed.'

'Well, I'm really sorry to hear that,' Albert said sympathetically. 'She was a good soul. I often said hello to her in Patel's shop. She'll be missed.'

'Oh, but it's worse than that,' Brenda went on, unable to conceal her eagerness to continue her report. 'She was in her late eighties. At least she'd had a good long life. But her younger son who lived at home with his mother, he's been taken to hospital this afternoon. I spoke to one of the neighbours who saw him being carried into the ambulance. They thought he looked very bad. Said they wouldn't give much for his chances of ever coming home again. You know I hate to be the bearer of bad news. But people need to know. We all need to be on our guard. It could snatch any of us away at any moment.'

Albert could see that Brenda Braithwaite would have continued in this vein indefinitely had he been willing to stay and listen. He politely and sincerely said how sorry he was to hear her news, encouraged her to keep safe, and resumed his journey home before she could extend the conversation any further. He was always a little irritated by folk who seemed to derive some kind of vicarious pleasure from the suffering of others. In his years as a postman he'd developed a technique for avoiding direct engagement with such people. He would push the mail through the letter box just slowly enough for it to balance and hang for a moment before falling on the other side of the door. That allowed him sufficient time to be halfway down the pathway before the occupant of the house, alerted by the sound of their letters dropping to the floor, could open the door and engage him in conversation. He often wished he could think of something that would be as effective for avoiding the kind of encounter he'd just been forced to endure.

It was a relief to reach the front door of number 77 Park Avenue and let himself into the house. He ran himself a warm bath and tried to work out exactly how he was feeling. He was tired and hungry after his day's work, he was cross at Brenda Braithwaite's prattling, and he was struggling and failing to shake off the sadness that had hung over him since Binu had told him of Pranav's death. This evening, however, he was aware of an unfamiliar sensation in his stomach that he couldn't ignore. People often remarked that he seldom seemed to worry about things. One of his old colleagues at the sorting office used to joke about him. 'You should be like Albert,' he'd tell any colleague who was fretting about something. 'Nothing ever worries him. Takes everything in his stride. Stridemore by name, Stridemore by nature.' But this evening Albert Stridemore *was* worried. Whether or not Brenda Braithwaite's concern was genuine, her news was troubling him.

Until now the 'Shawe had felt like an island, separated from the mainland by the Irmingshawe Road. The virus might be lurking unseen in other areas of the city and throughout the country. But the residents of the 'Shawe were solid, sensible, working-class people, canny folk who knew how to hunker down, knew how to look after themselves, knew how to look out for each other. And Pranav Patel was a doctor, for goodness' sake. He'd spent years studying medicine, learning how to fight infections and cure the sick. He was part of that army of people who worked on the front line of the National Health Service, winning battles against disease and rescuing victims from the jaws of death. But now the 'Shawe itself had been invaded by the virus and Dr Pranav Patel, one of its finest sons, was himself the latest casualty in this war. This was worrying, even for a man who took things in his stride.

Albert felt a little better after he'd eaten his dinner and dropped off to sleep for twenty minutes in the armchair. That was why he'd got so anxious, he told himself when he woke up. He'd allowed himself to get too hungry and overtired. Sitting at home and worrying never solved anything. He'd walk round to Patel's General Store and check how his friend was doing.

When he got to the shop, there were four or five people standing on the pavement observing the instruction on the proprietor's handwritten notice in the window that only two people were allowed inside at one time. Albert tagged on to the end of the queue and waited until it was his turn to enter. The other customer paid for her purchases and left him alone with Binu.

'How are you, my friend? I wondered if you might have closed early today.'

'Now, Albert Stridemore, how long have we been friends?' Binu sprayed the counter with sanitiser and wiped it clean as he spoke. 'You should know me better than that. I am getting on with what I should be doing – running my shop. It wouldn't be doing me any good at all to be sitting around moping. My loyal customers would be having to walk all the way to the supermarket where nobody has the time to ask them how they are. And I wouldn't have had the comfort of all my customers asking *me* how I am doing and offering me their sympathy.'

He spoke without a hint of self-pity and Albert had to pretend there was something in his eye to hide the tear that threatened to run down his cheek. For the second time that evening he tried to tell himself that what he was feeling was just the result of his tiredness. But he knew better. There had been moments like this before when Binu's dignified refusal to give way to anger or resentment had moved him deeply.

'You're a good man, Binu Patel. You don't deserve what's happened. But I am proud to be your friend.'

'I am still learning how to be good. But I am thinking that maybe it's a good thing that we don't always get what we deserve. And I, too, am glad that you are my friend.'

There were no more customers that evening. So Binu fetched a couple of chairs and they sat outside in the cool breeze until it was time for Binu to close the shop. They talked about the past, about how they'd come to know each other so many years before, about what life had been like when their children were young, and about how they both now knew what it was like to lose a son. It was the kind of conversation where the long silences were as important as the words they actually spoke to each other. The kind of conversation that only works between old friends who've come to appreciate each other's company as a greater gift than any wise counsel they can share. When they parted for the second time that day, it was with a promise to enjoy that gift for as long as they had breath in their bodies.

Albert arrived home feeling less troubled than when he'd set out an hour or so earlier and thinking he'd sleep all the better for the time he'd spent with Binu. He'd made a cup of tea and got into his pyjamas, intending just to sit quietly for a few minutes, when it occurred to him that he hadn't had time to catch up with what was happening in the world beyond the 'Shawe. A glance at the clock told him that he was just in time for the ten o'clock news on television and he decided that since he was so tired, he'd just watch the headlines before retiring for the night.

In fact, by the time he turned off the television at the end of the programme, he was an angry man. And, exhausted though he was, he knew he was in no mood to sleep.

The main item on the news had focused on the Prime Minister's senior advisor, Dominic Cummings, and the trip he'd made some weeks earlier with his wife and child from his home in London to a property owned by his parents in Durham. Albert did not particularly like what he'd read of the man or of the manner in which he was reputed to operate. And there was the matter of how he chose to dress at his place of employment. In his forty years as a postman, Albert had always prided himself in keeping his uniform smart and his shoes polished. 'After all,' he would say to a colleague he deemed careless about his appearance, 'we work for the Royal Mail and we represent Queen and country just as much as the armed forces do.'

Grudgingly, Albert conceded that the Britain in which he now lived was a much less formal place than the one he'd grown up in. And he'd come to accept, though he regretted it, that news reporters and doctors and politicians and people in other professions no longer bothered to wear a tie. But this man – it made Albert hot under the collar just thinking about it – *this man* arrived at Number 10 Downing Street, the Prime Minister's residence, the centre of government, not just in casual clothing, but looking as if he'd stuck glue on his body and run through a heap of discarded clothing!

'It just looks like he's sticking two fingers up at the rest of us,' he'd lament to Binu, who would smile benignly and tell him that it wasn't worth getting worked up about.

Maybe Binu was right about that. But Albert had followed this story from the beginning and he considered that what he'd just watched certainly *was* worth getting worked up about. He could remember clearly that back in the middle of March the Prime Minister had instructed everyone in the country to self-isolate for seven days if they believed they had any symptoms of the coronavirus. He'd specifically forbidden people to leave their home and stay somewhere else. But, in the last few days, the story had broken in the national press that less than a week after that announcement Mr Cummings had travelled more than 200 miles with his wife, who was unwell, and their four-year-old child to a property that his parents owned in Durham, claiming that they were unable to find anyone to care for their child in London. And while in Durham, having himself been unwell from the virus, he'd driven with his family to a nearby beauty spot at Barnard Castle thirty miles from Durham where he'd taken a short walk, even though most people understood that recreational outings like this were in breach of the guidelines. Mr Cummings had justified this trip by saying that he'd done it as a way of testing whether his eyesight, which had been affected by his illness, was sufficiently recovered for him to drive back to London the following day.

Albert knew that, like himself, the majority of people in the country as well as MPs from all the major parties had been totally unconvinced by Mr Cummings' explanations of his conduct. Despite the fact that he had the backing of the Prime Minister, such had been the extent of the demands for his resignation that he'd been forced to make a statement and answer questions in the garden of 10 Downing Street earlier in the day. But as the excerpts he'd just watched from that press conference made clear, far from offering his resignation, Mr Cummings had refused even to offer an apology, insisting that he didn't regret what he had done.

The exhaustion of a long day and the grief he felt for his friend fuelled the anger that welled up in Albert. Who did this man think he was? Had he no idea of what so many ordinary people who, unlike him, had no access to a second home in the countryside, had suffered during this lockdown? Didn't he understand that people had been forbidden to visit their loved ones in hospital? Or that thousands had died without a family member to hold their hand?

He got up and walked round the room several times, unable to contain his anger. He went outside and stood in his garden, shaking his head in sheer disbelief at what he considered the breath-taking arrogance of the man. He went back into the house and sat down at his computer. He'd send an email to his Member of Parliament, to the newspaper, to the local radio station, to anybody he could think of. Then he changed his mind and shut down his laptop. He knew just what he should do. He went into the kitchen and opened the drawer where he kept the fountain pen he'd been given as a retirement gift and the sheets of good-quality writing paper that he used only for letters about things that were really important. He made another cup of tea, sat at the kitchen table and began to write. It took him several attempts, but after an hour the letter was finished.

77, Park Avenue,
Irminghsawe Estate,
Manchester
M48
25th May 2020

The Rt Hon Boris Johnson
Prime Minister
c/o 10 Downing Street,
Westminster,
London
SW1A 2AA

Dear Prime Minister,
    I am a patriotic citizen and prior to my retirement I was proud to serve this country as a

postman with the Royal Mail for nearly forty years. I have always sought to be supportive of the government of the UK, whatever political party is in power and whoever occupies your office. I am sure that I was one of the many British people who were delighted to learn of your recovery from the coronavirus and I wish you continued good health.

However, I am writing to express my disappointment and, indeed, my anger at the way you seem to be condoning what most of us consider to be the irresponsible conduct of your advisor, Mr Cummings, in travelling to Durham during the lockdown. I believe that your unwillingness to condemn his actions and his failure to do the honourable thing and resign, or even apologise, has damaged your own credibility and the authority of your government. The impression that has been given is that there is one set of rules for those in power and another for the rest of us. I fear that this may well result in the people of this country being less willing to carry out any future guidelines you issue during this pandemic. Sadly, this may well result in a greater loss of life than would otherwise have been the case.

I doubt that you will change your mind on this matter, but I feel that I have done my duty as a good citizen in communicating what I and, I believe, the vast majority of the British public think about this.

Yours sincerely,

Albert Stridemore

He read it over two or three times, folded it carefully and slipped it into an envelope ready to be posted the next day. Within minutes after going to bed, he fell into a deep sleep. For the first time in his life he failed to wake up when his alarm sounded at seven o'clock in the morning.

# 10
# 6th June 2020
# Walking in Company

Albert rose at his usual time of seven o'clock on Saturday 6th June. He checked the weather forecast and was relieved to see that the early morning rain would give way to a drier and brighter afternoon. Then he washed and shaved, just as he always did. After that he made himself a hearty breakfast, which was something he did only on Saturdays, settling for a couple of slices of toast and a cup of tea for the rest of the week. But today was different from any that had gone before. He watched the bacon, eggs and sausage sizzling in the frying pan with a mixture of anticipation and nervousness at what the day would hold for him. Well, it wasn't often at his age that he would step outside his door knowing that he'd be doing something that he'd never done in his life before.

To be honest, he was really feeling too excited to sit down to breakfast, but he reckoned that there would be little chance to eat again until he got home late in the afternoon. He forced himself to eat slowly, hardly able to believe what he was about to do, how much his thinking had changed in a relatively short time, and how he'd reached the point of making a decision he wouldn't have believed possible a couple of weeks earlier.

It had all started on the morning of 27th May, the day after he'd written his letter to the Prime Minister. He'd got to bed so late the night before that he'd overslept and decided that he'd wait until the afternoon before going to his allotment. Only a few days earlier, he'd realised that he could access the BBC news channel on his laptop, which felt to him like a whole new window on to the world, and one that he could open at any time without waiting for the regular news bulletins on television.

Still intrigued by this discovery, he logged in before heading out for the rest of the day. That was when he saw the report of the death of George Floyd, a forty-six-year-old African American man, in Minneapolis the day before. Apparently, the police had been summoned by an employee of a grocery store who'd accused Floyd of trying to pay for his purchases with a forged $20 bill. It wasn't clear exactly what had happened after the police arrived, but the upshot was that Floyd had been pulled out of the back of a patrol car and onto the ground. Albert watched in horror at the video showing the police officer kneeling on the man's neck for almost nine minutes while Floyd repeated several times, 'I can't breathe.' According to the report, he was eventually taken by ambulance to a hospital where he was later pronounced dead.

Whether or not George Floyd had been guilty of a crime, Albert had no way of knowing. What was clear to him was that the level of force used by the police officer was out of all proportion to the nature of the crime he was accused of committing.

Apart from his shock at the level of police brutality in this case, his first reaction was one of relief that such things were so much less likely in Britain where the whole approach of a police force that wasn't routinely armed was completely different from that of America's law enforcement agencies. And, of course, while there were extremists on the far right of the political spectrum, Britain didn't have anything like America's problems of racial tensions.

But throughout that afternoon, as he worked quietly on his allotment, he couldn't erase from his mind the sickening image of a middle-aged man pinned to the ground by a police officer kneeling on his neck, unable to breathe, begging for his life and calling out for his mother. Was it possible, he wondered, that incidents like this happened more than he'd ever realised? It occupied his thoughts so much that he forgot to pick up his letter addressed to the Prime Minister at 10 Downing Street and drop it in the post on his way to his allotment that day. In fact, he never did send it. When he did remember it, he conceded that its intended recipient would in all likelihood never have read it and that all it would have achieved would have been a curt and formal reply from some junior member of staff in his office. But he felt better for having written it and hoped that one day Mr Cummings might give some thought to his odd manner of dress and his apparently high-handed actions.

That evening he was back on his computer again, surfing news websites and finding article after article about women and men on both sides of the Atlantic and in other white-majority countries who had disturbing stories to tell of how they'd been the victims of racial prejudice or had suffered unfair treatment at the hands of police officers or other authority figures they believed were racially biased.

He kept coming across the letters BAME. He'd seen them before, of course, but he'd passed over them without paying much attention. Just another of the thousand and one examples of the pretentious gobbledygook and confusing abbreviations that seemed to be infesting the Queen's English he'd been taught back in his school days. He wasn't sure if you were meant just to spell out each letter – B-A-M-E – or whether you pronounced it Bame so that it rhymed with name. Now he discovered it was an acronym for *Black, Asian and Minority Ethnic*, a catch-all reference to people who weren't of white descent.

The more reports he read and the more video clips he watched, the more he began to think that he'd been, albeit unintentionally, deaf and blind to much of what was going on around him every day. At ten o'clock, realising that if he wasn't careful he'd be sitting up later than he should for the second night in succession, he was just about to shut down his laptop when he came across another phrase he vaguely recognised but to which he'd never given much attention – *unconscious bias*. He'd heard it bandied around on current affairs programmes. It had often sounded to him like just another bit of clever jargon that people with more education than common sense used to score points over their opponents on the other side of the argument. But he was beginning to realise that there was a lot more to it than that.

He lay in bed that night remembering what he'd considered at the time to be the good-natured banter of his fellow postmen. As he thought about those days, however, he realised that most of that 'good-natured banter' had been directed towards two of his colleagues – one an immigrant from Pakistan and the other a man whose parents had come to the UK from the West Indies. It would usually take the form of joking comments about the colour of their skin, imitating how they spoke with their accent exaggerated for comic effect, or referring to them by names popularly used for people of colour that were considered funny back then but today would result in a formal complaint in any place of work. Albert had always felt slightly uneasy about it. But if anyone challenged it – though that rarely happened – the response would always be that it was just a bit of fun and wasn't any different from calling a Scotsman 'Jock' or a Welshman 'Taffy'. But it *was* different, and there were moments when the difference became all too clear. There were a few of his colleagues who were always reluctant to sit at the same table in the canteen as the men who were the butt of their jokes.

'It's not prejudice,' would be the response when anyone asked them about it. 'It's just that they don't have the same hygiene standards as English people.'

And there had been a general sense that there was no point in either of the men applying for promotion. They were acknowledged to be good workers and no trouble to have around, but everybody 'knew' they weren't cut out for anything that demanded more than physical strength and the ability to carry out instructions. It was an assumption to which, without giving it any real thought, he'd acquiesced. He consoled himself with the memory that he'd worked hard when he chaired the residents' association to ensure that people were treated fairly regardless of the colour of their skin or their ethnic origin. But he also recognised his attitude had generally been paternalistic rather than seeing them as equals.

Albert's discomfort became all the greater throughout the following week. Day after day he watched the news reports of demonstrations, not only in America but also in cities across the world, as the Black Lives Matter movement gained a new momentum. He was impressed that, although there were undoubtedly instances of disorder and even violence on the edges of these protests, they were largely peaceful and surprisingly dignified.

What challenged him most was an interview he saw with a young black man who said, looking straight at the camera, 'It's not enough to be able to say you're not racist. You need to be anti-racist.' It was a statement that had an immediate effect on him. He wasn't racist. At least, he didn't think he was. But he knew for certain that he hadn't been anti-racist. He'd never joined in what he now recognised as a kind of low-level racist abuse of his Asian and West Indian colleagues in the sorting office. But equally, he'd never spoken up against it.

If only he were younger, he thought to himself, he'd join one of those protests. It was a thought he managed to push to the back of his mind until he discovered that there would be a Black Lives Matter demonstration in Manchester on 6th June. Now he started to ask himself some very uncomfortable questions. What did his age have to do with anything? He'd always prided himself on being fit and healthy for his years. Always got annoyed with people who made their age an excuse for not keeping active and staying involved in life. So why was it different when it came to standing up and being counted in the face of an injustice so many people – himself included – had just ignored for so long? Why shouldn't he take part in the upcoming demonstration?

He spoke to Binu about it, who told him there was no reason why he shouldn't do it if he was feeling strongly about the matter. He would have been willing to close for a day and come with him, he said, if it wasn't for the fact that so many people on the 'Shawe needed the shop to be open.

'It's an issue that won't go away unless we are facing up to it. In my early years here, it wasn't uncommon to have a window broken or a racist slogan daubed on the wall outside. From time to time I am still hearing the occasional comment about my brown skin or my funny accent from the odd person who comes into the shop. And I've been around a long time and made a lot of friends among my customers.'

It was a casual-sounding comment and there wasn't a hint of anger in his voice, but it stopped Albert in his tracks. He'd never thought of Binu as being anything other than his friend and neighbour for so many years, a valued member of the 'Shawe community, a good and decent man. Certainly not an incomer or an intruder. And yet even Binu could still be on the receiving end of racial bigotry. Perhaps it *was* time to stand up and be counted.

'Why don't you call Mrs Finch?' Binu asked. 'She might be able to give you some wise counsel on this matter.

Though I'm thinking that you already know what you should be doing.'

Albert followed his friend's advice and called Penny Finch, told her what was in his mind and asked for her counsel. Was he just getting carried away by what he was seeing and hearing on the news? Had he been spending too much time online and getting things out of proportion? Did she think it was ridiculous for a white man in his mid-seventies to imagine he could be part of a Black Lives Matter demonstration? And what about the fact that they were in the middle of a pandemic and the government was strongly discouraging crowds from gathering because of the risk of increasing the transmission of the virus?

When he ran out of questions, he could hear Penny chuckling to herself at the other end of the phone.

'Well, well, Albert, you really have been getting worked up about this. Good for you. The virus is a real concern and normally my advice to anyone would be to avoid crowds at this time. But sometimes circumstances are such that we have to decide between two opposing choices, neither of which is completely right or wrong. So I certainly don't think you're being ridiculous. In fact, I've got a feeling you'd have a job forgiving yourself if you didn't go. Maybe this strange time is uncovering things about yourself you didn't even know were there. Maybe you've been self-isolating on your allotment for too long...'

'So you really think I should go?' he asked, before she could finish her sentence.

'Not only do I think you should go, but if you don't mind my company, I'll come with you. It would do me good, I'm sure. Now that I think about it, I haven't been on a protest since I took part in a CND march back in the early eighties.'

The result of their conversation was that among the twenty or so mainly young people who boarded the city-bound tram at the Irmingshawe Park Metro stop just before twelve o'clock on Saturday 6th June was an older couple – an upright elderly man wearing a navy-blue blazer with a Royal Mail badge embroidered on the breast pocket and his female companion, casually dressed in cotton slacks and a fashionable loose-fitting jacket, and looking younger than her seventy years. They were both wearing protective masks and doing their best, admittedly with only limited success, to keep as far as they could from other passengers and to maintain a distance of two metres from each other. It was a relief when the tram pulled into Piccadilly Gardens and the doors slid open, allowing them to step onto the platform and breathe the fresher outside air.

As a gardener, Albert had always thought that Piccadilly Square would have been a better name than Piccadilly Gardens. Admittedly, there was a stretch of well-worn grass to be seen if you looked hard enough, but surrounded as it was by city-centre buildings on three sides and a curving concrete wall on the fourth that made many Mancunians think of the worst excesses of Eastern Bloc architecture in the 1950s, Piccadilly *Gardens* was definitely a misnomer. He'd walked across it no more than three or four times in the last ten years and each time he'd thought what an unpleasant place it was.

Today, however, as he stood with Penny and watched it gradually fill with people – the majority of whom he was pleasantly surprised to see were wearing face masks – it felt very different. Many in the crowd were carrying banners with slogans, some referring back to the killing of George Floyd in America, and others looking forward and demanding greater justice and equal opportunities for people irrespective of the colour of their skin. He particularly liked one that carried the message, 'Racism is a pandemic too'. It perfectly expressed what he'd been increasingly realising and it helped ease the guilt he was still feeling for not obeying the lockdown guidelines. Defeating racism was as important as conquering the virus.

It was almost one o'clock and, as far as he could tell from where they were standing, everyone was behaving sensibly and there were no signs of any aggressive or violent conduct. He was certainly in the company of people with strong feelings about the issue of racial injustice. But there was something of a party atmosphere. The women and men around him had come not just to demonstrate, but also to celebrate. They'd come to celebrate life; to celebrate their common humanity with people of every colour and every ethnic group. And he was finding the experience invigorating.

He suddenly became aware that Penny was looking at him and smiling.

'I've got a feeling, Albert Stridemore, that you're enjoying yourself a lot more than you thought you would.

What d'you think? Is it going to be worth sacrificing a day on your allotment?'

'Well...' He paused for a moment as he surveyed the scene. 'I wasn't sure what to expect. But, to be honest, I haven't felt this young since I don't know when.'

Then something happened that changed the mood and brought an almost palpable hush to the proceedings. It started at the furthest point from Albert and Penny and moved slowly but irresistibly through the crowd until it reached them. It was as if some unseen hand was gently rippling an enormous silk sheet until it covered the entire square and settled on everyone. All across Piccadilly Gardens people stopped talking or chanting slogans and got down on one knee.

What had felt like a party just minutes earlier now seemed more like an act of worship. A time of repentance for past wrongs. A sign of respect for those who had suffered pain and injustice and even death. A solemn act of dedication to the cause of fighting racism and making the world a better place.

Albert had seen and read enough to understand the significance of 'taking a knee' to the Black Lives Matter movement. He had guessed it would happen, but he had not expected it to be quite so dignified and orderly as this. As people around them assumed the posture of prayer and humility, he asked Penny if she was OK to kneel. She smiled again and assured him that she certainly was. He produced a clean, white handkerchief from his jacket pocket for her to kneel on before he knelt beside her. And for two minutes, with only the hum of the city traffic in the background and a gentle breeze blowing across Piccadilly

Gardens, the place that he'd never liked had become for him an open-air cathedral.

The noise of more than 10,000 people getting back to their feet and preparing to parade through the city in peaceful protest was, if anything, even more moving than what had just gone before. It was a sound that made him think of an Old Testament story he'd known since childhood – Ezekiel's vision in which the dry bones scattered in the valley came to life and formed a vast army. And he was proud to be part of this army, proud of the young people around him, proud of sharing in what was good and decent in the human race.

He'd often had a pang of regret that National Service had come to an end before he'd reached the age at which he'd have been liable for conscription. He would have been honoured to have served his country in the armed forces. But today he had joined a crusading force, armed not with powerful weapons that would kill and destroy, but with a passion for justice that would surely bring equality and opportunity to those held captive by bigotry and oppression. He was fighting not just for Queen and country but also for his brothers and sisters in every nation.

He would have gone on conversing with himself in this somewhat grandiose manner indefinitely had he not been brought down to earth by a voice from behind him.

'My, you're looking proud, Mr Stridemore. I reckon you're really cut out for this kind of thing. I'll bet you used to cut a fine figure in your postman's uniform back in the day. But would you mind waiting for me instead of striding on ahead?'

He turned to see Penny a few feet behind him. She was carrying a home-made banner with the words 'No justice no peace' written roughly with a felt-tip pen on a square of cardboard pinned to a broom handle.

'Where did you get that?' he laughed. 'Talk about me! You really look the part.'

She pointed to the tall, young, black man walking beside her, who gave Albert a mock salute and a broad smile.

'I gave it to her. Been on so many demonstrations over the last few years when everybody there was the same age and the same colour as me. I was so pleased to see folk like you joining in that I just wanted to give it to your wife as a gift.'

Albert tried to explain that she wasn't his wife and that they were just good friends, but his voice was drowned out as the crowd around them began to chant, 'I can't breathe! I can't breathe!' He could see Penny laughing at his confusion and he realised that he was blushing with embarrassment. He kept walking and tried to look straight ahead.

The crowd edged its way slowly out of Piccadilly Gardens and along Market Street. When they turned into Deansgate, the long, straight road that cuts through the city from north to south, Albert gasped at the sight of the thousands marching in front of them with their banners and placards held aloft. He agreed with Penny, who said it would have been worth being there just to witness the scene.

But it was when they passed through St Peter's Square that the chants and songs became louder and the

143

atmosphere became infused with resonances of the past. Albert knew the history of this part of the city and the significance it held for the marchers. Two hundred years earlier, just a few yards from where their feet were treading today, it had been the site of the infamous Peterloo Massacre. A crowd of 60,000 people, peacefully protesting against the oppressive corn laws and demanding the right to vote, had been viciously attacked by a company of sabre-wielding hussars. Such had been the carnage that long before the day was over, the ground was strewn with the bodies of the dead and wounded, their discarded and broken banners lying beside them. Today the policing was sensitive, even supportive, of the demonstration, and there would be no repeat of those events. But the inequalities persisted and the echoes of that terrible day reverberated in the ongoing fight against the injustices that still made millions of people throughout the world feel like second-class citizens.

They were coming back into Piccadilly Gardens, having circled round the city centre, when Albert heard someone calling to them. He couldn't imagine who would recognise them in a crowd like this until he spotted the young woman with a microphone on the end of a two-metre pole standing beside a man with a camera on his shoulder. It was Jacqui Aldred, the television reporter they'd met when she'd come to look at the work they were doing in the 'Shawe with GGOSH.

'Well, look at you two! You turn up in the most unexpected places.' She seemed delighted to see them. 'I was going to contact you this coming week about a follow-up feature on your food bank and grow-your-own-veg initiative. But you're just what we need right now. We're filming material for a piece on the evening news. We've got several interviews in the can already. Mostly younger people, as you can guess. It'd be great to get something from you two. Would you mind?'

Albert protested that he didn't really have anything to say. But Penny insisted that since it had been his idea to come and that she was really just keeping him company, he was the one they should speak to. He noticed, as he'd done before, just how good she was at putting herself in the background and pushing someone else forward into the limelight. Reluctantly, he stepped to the side to allow the other marchers to pass and stood in front of the camera. He cleared his throat as he waited nervously for Jacqui's questions. In fact, there was only one, and it was short and to the point.

'What's persuaded you to come out and join what many people think of as a movement of young people?'

'Well, I've noticed quite a few people of my age here today. And I think most of them are probably like me. Seeing and hearing what these young people have been doing over the past while has made me sit up and take notice. Face up to my responsibility, if you like. If our generation had done a better job at dealing with prejudice and bigotry, they wouldn't need to come out on the streets like this. So the least we can do is join them and give our support.'

He waited a little nervously for the second question, but it never came.

'That's it,' Jacqui Aldred said after a pause. 'You've nailed it. That'll fit perfectly into our piece. In fact, it'll round it off nicely. And, Mrs Finch, I'll be in touch during the week about coming over to the 'Shawe again.'

As they rejoined the marchers filing back into Piccadilly Gardens, Penny nodded approvingly at Albert.

'Well done. You really don't need to be nervous about things like that. You're better at it than you think.'

He blushed for the second time that day, and he was really grateful when she quickly looked the other way and pretended not to notice.

The marchers gradually dispersed and Albert and Penny made their way to the tram stop, only to find that not only was it already crammed, but that there was also a queue of people who couldn't even get on to the platform stretching more than a 100 yards. To Albert's surprise, Penny suggested that they should walk home.

'But it's a good eight miles,' he protested. 'And you've already walked a fair distance.'

'I know. But it's a decent afternoon and it'll be a lot healthier than travelling in a crowded tram for the second time today. I've got comfortable shoes on and walking's no trouble to you.'

Since the moment he'd driven out of Bornaby and set off for Manchester, Albert had walked alone. He'd walked alone every working day on his round as a postman; he'd walked alone since he'd retired, making his way to and from his allotment; he'd walked alone on the long treks he'd taken by the side of Manchester's canals or on his visits to some of the most beautiful and loneliest regions in the north of England. Walking alone defined who he was. It had become a kind of metaphor for his life. Of course, he mixed with other people. He knew how to be courteous and companionable. He involved himself in the life of the community on the 'Shawe. He valued the friendship of Binu. But still, he walked alone. The people around him were like the folk he'd encounter on his walks. Sometimes they'd step aside to let him pass, sometimes they'd stop briefly and share a greeting, sometimes they might even fall into step with him for a mile or so before they said goodbye and parted. And he would stride out again, grateful for their company but glad to be free, unencumbered by any entanglement, unthreatened by the fear of the hurts that might come from getting too close to anyone.

Now, however, he was walking the eight miles from the city centre back to the 'Shawe in the company of someone who was six inches shorter than he was, who took much smaller footsteps and who walked considerably more slowly than he did. At first, it was an exercise in concentration as he constantly forced himself to alter his pace and adjust his stride to accommodate the woman by his side. After the first mile, however, almost without realising it, he did something he couldn't remember ever doing before. He stopped striding and began to stroll, letting Penny set the pace and allowing himself to relax. And then something else happened that he hadn't expected. *He actually found himself enjoying it.* There was time and breath enough for conversation. Not discussion or debate or deliberation about which route to follow. Just conversation. And not about anything in particular. But about everything in general. Conversation that even the masks they were wearing couldn't inhibit. Conversation that flowed until they both realised just how hungry they were and stopped at a newsagent-cum-general store where they bought two bottles of water, two apples, two packs of sandwiches and two blueberry muffins.

Still keeping two metres apart, they sat on a low wall just outside the shop, took off their masks and ate and drank together. Between mouthfuls, they laughed at how hungry they were feeling and how good the plainest food tastes when you're really hungry. And, when they'd finished eating and drinking, Albert gathered up the litter and carefully put it in the nearby waste bin. For anyone passing by it would have seemed the most unremarkable scene. Two people eating takeaway food on the outskirts of the city centre on a Saturday afternoon. Albert, however, thought it had been one of the most memorable and enjoyable meals he'd ever eaten.

They set off for home again, chatting as naturally as they had been before they stopped. The further they walked, however, the less they talked. Much of that was down to the fact that they were growing limb-weary after what had turned out to be a longer day than they'd anticipated. But there was more to their silence than tiredness. It was Penny who put into words what Albert had already been thinking to himself.

'We haven't known each other all that long,' she remarked, when they paused to take a rest and gather their strength for the last mile of their journey. 'But it's nice when you reach a point at which you're comfortable enough in each other's company that you don't feel the need to talk. That's the mark of a real friendship, I always think.'

He readily agreed. And, if he'd hadn't felt so tongue-tied, he would have added that normally it took him a long time to get to know anyone well. Even then, his relationships were never close. Most of the people he knew were more acquaintances than real friends. Binu, of course, was the one great exception, though they'd never socialised together in the way that most friends would. They almost always met in the mornings as Binu was getting ready to open the shop or late in the evening when he was closing up for the day. For all that, it was a friendship that meant a lot to them both. But this was different.

He would have shared his thoughts if he hadn't been overcome by a fear that his words would come out all wrong and blight their growing friendship before it had time to blossom. So he smiled and nodded and contented himself with enjoying the silence to which she'd just referred as they walked on together.

It was after eight o'clock when they reached Penny's house. They stood by the gate for a moment, reflecting on what an exhausting but pleasant day they'd had together. Out of nowhere, he had a sudden mental image of himself as a sixteen-year-old, standing at Maureen Watson's gate and saying goodbye. Back then he'd felt awkward and hadn't been sure what to do. And he felt just as awkward and just as uncertain now. It was years since anything had caused him to blush. Now he could feel the colour rising in his cheeks for the third time that day. Yet again, he was sure Penny Finch knew exactly what was happening. And yet again she came to the rescue.

'If I'm not careful, I'm going to start yawning. It's time for my beauty sleep. And you look pretty well done in too, Albert Stridemore. Thank you for today.'

She stepped a little closer and patted his hand before she turned and walked up the path. Just as she got to the door, she turned and added with a wink, 'Oh, and thanks for walking at my pace. Very gallant of you.'

Albert responded with a gesture that was halfway between a cheery wave and a smart salute. He waited until she'd opened the door and let herself into her house before taking a deep breath and striding purposefully towards the 'Shawe.

It had been a good day. A day of new experiences and long-forgotten emotions. He was too tired to figure out what it all meant or why he felt so pleased about everything. For now, all he wanted was to be home, get to bed and enjoy a good night's sleep.

# 11
# 13th June 2020
# Bubble-wrapped

It was three o'clock in the afternoon on Saturday 13th June when Albert Stridemore arrived on the doorstep of number 5 Irmingshawe Road for the second time in a month. Just as on his last visit, he was holding an armful of flowers picked from his garden. This time, however, the bunch was twice as big as before and the array of blooms was even more extravagant and colourful. There were geraniums and astrantias and irises and dahlias and penstemons, and half a dozen other varieties all wrapped up in some crinkly pink paper he'd bought specially from Patel's General Store the previous evening.

And, as anyone from the 'Shawe who'd happened to see him that afternoon would have noticed immediately, Albert himself was looking different. Gary Hill at number 79 Park Avenue had been surprised when his next-door neighbour had leaned over the fence one afternoon to ask for his advice on what he should wear for what he described as 'just a casual day out with a friend who's a little bit younger than I am'. The Hills had often been the beneficiaries of Albert's gifts of produce from the allotment and Gary was grateful for the opportunity to do something in return for his neighbour's generosity year after year. He emailed a list of suggestions to Albert – complete with photos – gave him the details of where he could order the items online, and promised that Eileen, his wife, would gladly make any adjustments needed to ensure that everything fitted perfectly.

So this afternoon Albert had left his three tweed jackets and four pairs of flannels hanging in the wardrobe. Instead, he was wearing a pair of olive-coloured chinos, a short-sleeved white shirt with a button-down collar, and a charcoal-grey sweater slung over his shoulders. Eileen Hill had shown him how to tie the sleeves loosely across his chest – 'So it doesn't end up looking like a scarf,' she'd explained – and he'd practised the manoeuvre several times in front of the mirror in his bedroom to make sure he'd got it right.

His one concession to his normal mode of dress was the pair of brown brogues on his feet. To wear any other style of shoe, he insisted, would be 'a step too far' for him. He was a little annoyed by Gary and Eileen's barely concealed amusement at that statement, though he did join in their laughter when he realised what he'd said. He remained adamant on his choice of footwear, however. In the end, with a little persuasion, he'd agreed to compromise by choosing a natty pair of *suede* brogues. And now that he'd got used to them, he had to admit that he rather liked how they looked.

For all his careful preparation, he was nervous as he rang the bell and waited for Penny to answer the door. This was no ordinary social visit. On Wednesday evening of that week, the members of the GGOSH steering committee had held their fortnightly meeting, standing in a circle on the pavement in front of Patel's General Store. After they'd completed their business and were getting ready to go their separate ways, someone had mentioned the Prime Minister's announcement earlier in the day. The concerns being expressed by many experts about the negative effects of loneliness on mental health had led to the decision to ease the lockdown regulations for people who were living on their own. From Saturday onwards, the Prime Minister had stated, they would be permitted to form what he labelled 'a social bubble' with one other household. And the authorities would consider everyone in the bubble to be part of the same group, which would mean that the rules about social distancing would not apply.

There was general agreement among the members of the GGOSH steering committee that this was a positive move. But for two of their number the news of this change had been of more than passing interest. They'd caught each other's eye as the topic was being discussed, though neither of them had said anything. Later that evening, however, after a great deal of thought, Albert had written an email.

*Penny,*

*I'm not sure if I'm doing the right thing by writing to you like this. But I thought it would be better to raise the matter in an email rather than face to face and risk putting you in an awkward situation. Please feel free just to ignore this email if you think that what I'm suggesting isn't a good idea. I give you my word that I won't ever bring the subject up again.*

*I've been thinking about this bubble thing. And I wondered if it might be something you'd consider trying since both of us are living on our own. I want to assure you that I've no intentions other than continuing to enjoy our friendship which has become really important to me in the last little while. And I give you my word that I would be very careful about protecting your good reputation. We'd obviously be careful not to stay late in each other's houses. I wouldn't want to give the local gossips something to talk about.*

*If I'm speaking out of turn, please accept my apologies. And, as I say, I won't mention it again.*
*Albert*

He decided not to send it straight away but to sleep on it and see if he still thought it was a good idea in the morning. But he kept going over it in his mind and he couldn't get off to sleep for thinking about it. So, at half past one in the morning, he got up, rewrote a couple of sentences, checked it for spelling and grammar, walked round the room a few times and then hit the 'send' button.

He woke early after a restless night, still thinking about his email and telling himself that he'd probably made a big mistake in sending it. What if he'd offended her? What if she was so annoyed by what he'd suggested that she never wanted to speak to him again? What if she told someone else about it? It would get round the 'Shawe in no time and he'd be a joke.

It was half past nine before he plucked up the courage to turn on his laptop and check the inbox. There was a reply from Penny! He closed his eyes, afraid to look at it. But, unable to put it off any longer, he took a deep breath, opened his eyes and began to read.

> *Albert,*
>
> *Thank you for your email. Judging from the time at the top (1.44), I'm guessing that you must have thought about it a lot before you actually sent it. The funny thing is that I was still awake when it arrived. And though I didn't have my laptop on and didn't read it until I got up this morning, I was thinking pretty much the same way as you obviously were at half past one this morning!*
>
> *I'd be very happy to form a bubble with you. I'm not sure if 'form a bubble' is the right way to say it, but you know what I mean. Give me a call when you get this email and we can talk about it.*
>
> *Thank you for being so gentlemanly and thoughtful in the way you made the suggestion. Thanks, too, for being concerned in case my reputation might be damaged by our friendship. I think I've got to know you well enough, even in this short time, to know there's no danger of that happening.*
>
> *Love,*
> *Penny*

In all his life he'd never felt more relieved. He sat back in his chair and read it another three or four times, just to be sure he wasn't imagining it, before he logged off and prepared to get on with his day.

Half an hour later, walking through the park on the way to his allotment, he spotted Brenda Braithwaite coming towards him and wondered what tale she intended to regale him with this time that might delay him on his journey. But, on this occasion, she merely smiled, remarked on how happy he looked and observed that she couldn't ever recall having heard him whistling like he was doing today. He politely returned her greeting, relieved to be on his way without the expected interruption. He didn't tell Brenda the reason for his high spirits or that he'd been completely unaware that he was whistling until she commented on it.

Now, as he waited for Penny Finch to open the door, he heard himself whistling again. The passing of the years had taught him to be contented. Yes, there had been painful episodes in his past and things had not turned out as he'd anticipated when he was in his early twenties. But he'd learned to accept his lot in life and to be grateful for what he had. He was totally unaccustomed, however, to the waves of happiness that had been sweeping over him for the past few days. And the ongoing effect of his near-euphoria continued to take him by surprise. He resolved to be on his guard against any sudden temptation to break into song while walking through the 'Shawe. Whistling without being aware of it was bad enough. Singing in public might lead to concern among his neighbours for his mental well-being.

'Well, who should I find standing on my doorstep bearing a veritable abundance of flowers but my bubble partner, Albert Stridemore himself? And with a new smart-casual wardrobe, I see.' Penny swung the door wide open and stood back to allow him to enter. 'Welcome to our government-approved mutual household where social distancing can be forgotten and face masks temporarily discarded.'

He followed her through the hallway to the kitchen and set the flowers down on the table.

'I hope I haven't brought too many,' he said, wondering if there was some kind of protocol relating to how many flowers a gentleman should bring on his first visit to a lady's house.

'You can never bring too many flowers,' she replied, as she began to separate them out and place them in the half-dozen vases she'd lined up ready for his arrival. 'I was hoping you'd bring some of your magnificent blooms. I'm well prepared, as you can see. The ones you brought when we had lunch in the garden were beautiful. But, you know, I think these might be even nicer.'

As she busied herself arranging the flowers, she questioned him about the different varieties and how he managed to grow them so successfully. He guessed that, besides being genuinely interested in the answers, she reckoned that getting him to talk about a subject on which he was knowledgeable would be a good way to help him overcome his awkwardness at being in her home for the first time. If that was her intention, it worked well. After ten minutes, the conversation was flowing as naturally as it had done when they'd walked home from the Black Lives Matter demonstration. At her invitation, he followed her from room to room as she carefully placed the flowers where she thought they'd be seen to the best advantage.

'I'm never sure if men are as interested in seeing other people's houses as women are,' she said, when the task and the impromptu tour were completed and they returned to the kitchen. 'But I always think it's a good way of helping guests to feel at home. And, after all, you're more than just another guest. You're my bubble companion.'

Albert smiled at that description and tried to assure her that he really had appreciated her showing him around. She raised her eyebrows and looked a little dubious, however, and asked him if he was just being nice to her.

'No, I *did* enjoy it,' he insisted. 'Don't forget, I was a painter and decorator once. It was a long time ago, I know, but I still have an eye for how things look. I really do like your house. It's restful and homely. And it's very... well, very *you*. I mean, it doesn't look like you've just followed the latest fad or copied something you've seen in some magazine. It's different... interesting. And I love all the pictures and ornaments that you've obviously gathered over the years. It's like after your busy working life you've found a place to rest and settle down.'

'Well, you've got that right. A place to rest and settle down. Couldn't have put it any better myself. And, since you approve, let's make some tea and take it through to the lounge. It'll be nice just to sit and chat with someone after all these weeks on my own with nobody else coming in to enjoy the house with me.'

Being from a generation where it was considered good manners for a gentleman to keep his jacket on when he went out to someone's home for dinner, Albert wasn't quite sure if the same rule applied to a sweater hanging over your shoulders. But, since he was getting warm and Penny had already remarked on how casual he was looking, he decided it was OK to remove it and hang it on the back of a kitchen chair before he picked up the tray that she'd set out, and carried it to the lounge.

They settled themselves in the leather armchairs on either side of the fireplace and drank tea. They talked about the undeniable disadvantages and the unexpected delights of life in lockdown. They discussed the progress of GGOSH, their surprise at just how many families living on the 'Shawe needed the help of a food bank, and their astonishment at how many had taken up Albert's challenge and were following his advice on growing their own vegetables. They reminisced about things they remembered from growing up in the 1950s and how living in those more austere times meant that they'd learned early in life never to take too much for granted. They reflected on how unpredictable life could be and how painful events that left you bruised could sometimes make you a better person. And they spoke at length about how odd their growing friendship might look to others and, indeed, how unlikely it seemed to them.

'I was a bit worried when I invited you to come for lunch last month that you might think I was some kind of merry widow trying to get my clutches into you,' Penny said. She was smiling, but he could see that it was a serious comment. 'I was afraid that it might scare you off.'

'That never occurred to me,' Albert laughed. 'But I couldn't work out why a professional woman like you wanted the company of someone like me. You've had a good education and a proper career. I'm just a retired postman who left school at fifteen. I'd no idea what we might have in common.'

'Well...' She hesitated, as if she wasn't quite sure how frank she could be. 'I wasn't thinking about what we had in common. Or even about friendship at first, to be honest. I was really interested in what made you so *different* from me. I don't mean the school you'd gone to or the job you'd done. It was a bit deeper than that. Since I retired, I've been trying to find myself again. My working life was so busy for years. I'm trying to figure out who exactly I am and what comes next, if that doesn't sound too affected. But you impressed me as a man who'd set his course in life and who was heading steadily in the direction he knew he should go. You seemed at ease with yourself. That fascinated me. To be truthful, I was a little envious of you.'

'Wow! Are you sure you've got the right person?' Albert shook his head in disbelief at what he'd just heard. He wasn't sure how to respond to a compliment like that. 'I suppose I can see what you're saying. But it's not quite what you seem to think. I told you my story last time we met. And all I've done is come to terms with how things are. I wanted to be a good husband, but my marriage ended up on the rocks. I wanted to be a good father, but I managed to mess that up. I didn't have enough ambition to go after promotion when I was given the opportunity. Some men end up drinking and trying to drown their sorrows when things go wrong. At least I didn't go down that blind alley. But I sometimes think that I've lived a second-best kind of life. I found a job that kept me on the move and stopped me from thinking too much about what might have been. And then I discovered the pleasure of growing things…'

He could see that Penny was listening intently and it unnerved him. But he couldn't just leave the conversation hanging there.

'I've found a lot of solace in turning over the soil and planting seeds and helping things grow. Gives me some hope that my life means something, that I've made some sort of contribution that will justify my time here. But there are times when I think that all my life amounts to is walking and digging. Just walking and digging. If I ever write my autobiography, maybe that's what I should call it. It pretty well sums me up. Maybe I'm hoping to keep on walking until I get somewhere. Or to keep on digging until I unearth a pot of gold that'll make me rich.'

In the wake of the confessions they'd just made to each other, a sombre kind of silence settled on the room. The only sound came from the footsteps of someone passing by on the street outside. They looked at each other across the lounge, neither of them sure what to say next. Then, quite spontaneously and at precisely the same moment, they both began to laugh. It was the kind of laughter that left Albert gasping for breath and Penny reaching for a tissue to dab her eyes and stop the tears running down her face.

'Oh my, what a pair of old miseries we are!' she said, hardly able to speak for laughing. 'If anyone could hear us, they'd wonder what kind of bubble this is.'

'I think they'd tell us to burst our bubble,' Albert responded, unable to resist the pun. 'Stop moaning and get on with things.'

'And that's exactly what I should be doing. Getting on with things.' She picked up the padded footstool that was sitting by the hearth and put it in front of his armchair. 'I need to go and make sure our dinner is cooking alright. Why don't you put your feet up for half an hour? I'm sure you could do with a nap.'

Living on his own for as long as he had done, Albert wasn't accustomed to being looked after like this, but he willingly accepted her suggestion. He drifted off to sleep, thinking to himself that it wouldn't be too difficult to get used to this kind of life.

Half an hour later, he woke up to the smell of Penny's home-cooking drifting into the room. He knew how to look after himself and he never failed to cook a proper dinner every day. But he'd forgotten how nice it was when someone else did the cooking. He took a deep breath and savoured both the aroma of the food and the pleasure of the moment. But it was the sound of Penny singing softly to herself as she pottered around in the kitchen, putting the finishing touches to the meal, that touched him deeply and reminded him of what he'd been missing all these years. Some of his neighbours on the 'Shawe, observing his fierce independence and self-sufficiency, often assumed that he was the kind of person who was naturally cut out for a life of singleness. The truth was, he'd learned to cope only by long practice and sheer willpower. And, as he lay back in the comfortable armchair with his feet on the stool, he recognised at what cost he'd succeeded.

He opened his eyes to see her standing at the door of the lounge and smiling at him. From her expression, he suspected that she'd been smiling at him for some time.

'Good, you're awake. Dinner is ready when you are, sir. It's a pleasant afternoon, so I thought we could eat in the garden like we did last time, if that's alright with you.'

Albert often needed to sleep for half an hour when he got home from his allotment before he ate his evening meal, and he'd come to believe that one of life's great verities was that nothing sharpens the appetite like a pre-dinner nap. It was a truth that held good for him now. Penny explained that she'd made what she called 'Balmoral Chicken', something she'd adapted from a meal she'd once enjoyed in a very expensive hotel in the Highlands of Scotland.

'It's chicken, thinly sliced – but not too thinly – wrapped around a haggis stuffing and served with roast potatoes, roast carrots, peas and broccoli and good meaty gravy. It's easy to make and I've done it lots of times when I've had guests. They always seem to enjoy it. You can tell me honestly what you think. And it goes down very nicely with a glass of red wine.'

Apart from saying 'Mmm' and 'Oh, yes' at regular intervals Albert didn't give a considered opinion until he'd cleared his plate, polished off an extra helping of Balmoral Chicken and drained his second glass of wine, which was one more than he normally permitted himself. Only then did he push his chair back from the table and deliver his verdict on the meal.

'Now, that was superb. Absolutely delicious. I take back all I've ever said about haggis being food fit only for

Highland cattle and Scotsmen who've had too much to drink. Seriously, that was a great meal. You're an excellent cook.'

His attempts to help clear the table and carry the plates back into the kitchen were immediately blocked by Penny who insisted that, as her guest, his sole responsibility was to eat and enjoy what was set in front of him. It was an instruction he was happy to obey when she produced a large bowl of fruit salad, a generous cheese board and a pot of freshly brewed coffee to complete what felt to him like a banquet fit for a king. If this was life in a bubble, he liked it!

They lost track of the time as they sat and talked. And, most of all, they gratefully basked in the warm glow of a friendship that had sparked into life without either of them having consciously tried to ignite the flame.

It was eight o'clock before the chill of the evening made them aware of how much time had passed and reminded Albert of his promise to protect the reputation of his hostess.

'I could sit and chat like this all night,' he said, easing himself up from his chair. 'But I should be going. I don't want to overstay my welcome on my first visit. A bubble's a fragile thing, after all.'

'Yes, it is,' Penny replied thoughtfully.' But I think this is a bit more like that bubble-wrap material you get to put round things to send through the post. You know, the stuff that cushions and protects valuable things that are breakable. I think what we're doing is more like that. But, if we're not careful, we'll be here trading puns and swapping similes all night.'

'That certainly wouldn't do,' Albert replied. 'But this has been a real treat for me. I don't remember when I last enjoyed myself so much.'

'Me too. And I'd love it if we could meet at your place next time we do this.'

There definitely would be a next time, they agreed; it would be at 77 Park Avenue and Albert would do the cooking. They walked to the front door and, just for a brief second or two, as he was about to leave, he wondered if he should give his hostess a quick peck on the cheek. It was a thought he quickly dismissed. That would be quite the wrong thing to do. It might send out the wrong signal and scare her away. This was a blossoming friendship between two older people who were just enjoying each other's company. Not a courtship between two giddy youngsters looking for romance. So, thinking that he couldn't just walk away, he reached out as if to shake hands and then withdrew his hand quickly as he couldn't remember what rules still applied to contact within a social bubble. He was relieved when that set them both off laughing and allowed him to cover up his rising embarrassment. Why he found himself blushing so often these days, he couldn't think.

What should have been no more than a ten-minute walk back home took more than an hour. Instead of striding out as he would typically have done, he was happy to walk at a little more leisurely pace, content to step out at what would have been for most folk a normal speed. Then he slowed to a stroll and, by the time he reached the edge of the 'Shawe, he was actually ambling along – with his hands in his pockets! *Albert Stridemore never put his hands in his pockets*. He usually got annoyed when he passed people walking with their hands in their pockets. Wanted to tell them to smarten up. But here he was, doing exactly that. Maybe, he thought to himself, he was on the inevitable downward spiral that begins when a man decides to dispense with his jacket and flannels and dress casually. But if that was the case, he really didn't care. In fact, for the first couple of hundred yards after he'd left Penny Finch's house, he'd been whistling.

And now, as he reached Patel's General Store, he was *singing*. Not out loud or anything as ridiculous as that. Just softly to himself. But, if anyone had challenged him about it, there was no way he could have denied that he'd been singing. He could have been making the song up as he was going along, but he thought it was one he vaguely remembered from the fifties or sixties. There was something about the moon standing still over a hill, though he'd forgotten the name of the hill. Which meant that he couldn't quite get the words to fit the tune. But that didn't bother him at all. And he was much too happy to think of going home yet.

That morning he'd told Binu that he and Penny had agreed to be 'bubble partners' – that was the best description of their new relationship he could think of – half-expecting that he'd disapprove. He'd been pleasantly surprised, however, when his friend had responded positively. So the least he could do now, he reasoned, was to give him a brief report of how his visit had gone. He pushed the door open and stepped inside, pleased to see that, apart from the proprietor himself, the shop was empty.

'Ah, it's my good friend, Albert Stridemore.' Binu looked at him questioningly. 'You're looking more than usually pleased with yourself, so I'm thinking that your time with Mrs Finch has gone well.'

Albert gave him almost a full report of his visit, omitting only the details of their conversations, which he thought were too personal even to be shared with his oldest friend.

'To be honest,' he concluded, 'I don't quite know what to make of it all. You and I have known each other for such a long time. You've been the only close friend I've had since I moved here fifty years ago. I never thought, especially at this stage of life, that there would be a place in my life for another friendship. I think I'm discovering things about myself I didn't know were there.'

'I think you probably are,' Binu responded, narrowing his eyes. 'Yes, I think you probably are. And I'm not sure you've got to the end of your discoveries yet.'

Albert wasn't sure what to make of that remark. But before he could think of a suitable answer, Binu reached to the sweet counter behind him and handed a packet of chewing gum over the counter.

'This is on the house. I can't imagine you ever putting this stuff in your mouth, but I'm giving it to you because it inspired me to think of a better name for your new friendship than bubble partners. I am proposing you call yourselves – are you ready for this? – *bubble chums*!'

Tickled by his own flair for the English language, Binu chuckled to himself at his wordplay. He'd obviously been anticipating this moment for some time. Albert, who always found his laughter infectious, readily joined in and accepted the unexpected gift. But his amusement quickly gave way to a contrasting emotion.

'How do you do it, Binu?' he asked, when he stopped laughing. 'I mean, I know how deeply you must be feeling the loss of Pranav. And yet you still find the energy from somewhere to share my enjoyment and think of a silly joke.'

Instead of replying immediately, Binu walked across the shop, locked the door and turned the sign around to show they were closed. Then, still without speaking, he went into the back room, brought out two chairs, positioned them two metres apart and invited Albert to sit opposite him.

'Now I will answer your question. Maybe you are not the only one who's discovering things about himself in these days. I am learning that it's possible to be very sad without being unhappy. Of course, I am grieving the loss of my son. I will be grieving for him as long as I live. But I am proud of who he was and what he did with his life and how he died. You and I disagree about what we hope and believe will happen after death. But we both agree that death is part of life and it is the step we will all have to take at some point. I would have wished that I would have taken that step long before Pranav. But that is not to be. Life goes on. We must live with things as they are, not as we would like them to be. And, because we are friends, you in the midst of your happiness share my grief, and I in the midst of my grief share your happiness.'

Albert wished he could say something appropriate, something that would adequately encapsulate his respect for his friend. But he could think of nothing more than, 'You're a good man, Binu Patel. And I'm glad I know you.'

By the time he left the shop and took the short walk home, the elation he'd been feeling all day had subsided and given way to a quiet sense of gratitude. To be fit and healthy at his age, particularly in a season of pandemic when people younger than he was had died before their time, was in itself a reason to be thankful. And to have the faithful friendship of the man whose presence he'd just left was a blessing that many would envy. But the company of Penny Finch was something completely unexpected. He smiled as he remembered what Binu had called it. They were bubble chums. And he could wish for nothing more than that.

# 12
## 21st June 2020
## Zooming in on Father's Day

Albert had never liked Father's Day. It brought back too many painful memories and bitter regrets that he kept buried throughout the rest of the year. He knew it was definitely not a day to be observed by a man like himself. A man who'd forfeited the right to be called a father. And he consoled himself with the thought that even if he'd had a dozen sons and daughters who looked up to him and visited him every week of his life, he still wouldn't have any enthusiasm for Father's Day. It wasn't a *proper* event on the national calendar. Not like Mothering Sunday that seemed to have some history and some real meaning to it. Father's Day, on the other hand, had obviously been dreamed up by an ambitious employee at a struggling greetings card company who'd been instructed by the boss to find a way of boosting flagging sales in the middle of summer. So, every year when the date came round again, he'd either head straight to his allotment first thing in the morning or get right out of Manchester and go for a long walk on his own where he wouldn't have to talk to another living soul.

This morning, however, his normal routine had been abandoned at the insistence of his bubble chum, and he was neither tending his plants nor striding along a lonely country lane. Instead, he was enjoying breakfast with Penny, who thoroughly approved of and had happily adopted Binu's description of their newly established relationship. Bubble chums summed it up perfectly. That, she agreed, was exactly what they were. Nothing more, nothing less. And when the country eventually emerged from lockdown and things got back to normal, they could decide where to go from there.

'You might be sick of the sight of me by then,' she laughed, as she served up breakfast. 'And if that's the case, you can cross to the other side of the street when you see me coming. But in the meantime, let's just enjoy each other's company.'

Originally they had agreed that Albert should cook breakfast at his house on the 'Shawe. But Penny had suddenly had a change of mind and had been really anxious that they should switch the venue to 5 Irmingshawe Road again so that he could meet her son.

'It'll only be a virtual visit, of course,' she'd explained. 'We still can't go and see him yet. They've got a strict no-visitor policy and so far they've been able to keep the home virus-free. But I call him once during the week and every Sunday. And Father's Day is important to him. He still misses his dad and he'll really appreciate talking to a man like you. He loves anything to do with gardens and plants. But I should warn you, he'll ask you a hundred and one questions. So you'd better have the answers ready.'

Since their visit would have to be online, Albert couldn't see why that couldn't have taken place equally well at his home. But Penny had been surprisingly insistent that it would work better if she provided breakfast. Reggie would be much more at ease if he could see the photos and ornaments in the background that he recognised, she explained. Especially when he was meeting someone new for the first time. Albert still wasn't fully convinced by her reasoning, but he thought it wasn't worth the risk of falling out over the issue this early in their friendship. And to add to his discomfort, the last thing he felt qualified for was the role of a substitute father figure to a disabled middle-aged man. That needed someone with skills he was sure he didn't possess. But, in the end, he'd agreed because he felt it was the kind of thing that she had a right to expect from someone who'd been bold enough to invite her to be his bubble chum. And now that he was here, tucking into a full English breakfast, he was feeling relaxed and glad he'd said yes to her request. He wasn't prepared, however, for Penny's next suggestion.

'Binu was telling me the other week what a strange man you are. He said that you go to church just once every year on Easter Sunday. That really amused him. But what about coming with me this morning while we eat?'

Going to church while eating breakfast seemed like a contradiction in terms to Albert. Surely doing one of those things made it impossible to do the other. But, as he suspected, Penny had something up her sleeve.

'I guess you might not have heard about what Olivia Smithers, the vicar of St George's, has been doing,' she continued as she opened up her laptop and set it up facing them on the kitchen table. 'I'm assuming that you won't have been logging on each week. But Olivia's got some of the younger folk in the congregation who know about this kind of thing helping her to do a ten o'clock Sunday morning service online during lockdown. They had some hiccups with the technology for the first couple of weeks, but they've pretty well managed to iron those out now. They're doing a good job. See what you think.'

Albert was initially dubious. While he'd learned to appreciate the value of the internet in recent months, mixing digital technology and religion seemed a step too far. Watching a service on a computer screen just wouldn't feel like church. But, since he was only halfway through his breakfast and he still hadn't done what he'd come to do, he knew there was no chance of escape.

To his surprise, he rather enjoyed it. The hymns were a mixture of new songs and old favourites he'd known since childhood, the prayers were done by some of the children in the church, the vicar gave a short talk, appropriately based on the story of the Good Samaritan, about the opportunities to be helpful to those in need, and there was a three-minute video showing some of the positive things that were happening on the 'Shawe. There was even a clip of two residents who'd been following Albert's gardening tips proudly holding up their home-grown carrots and potatoes. And the section devoted to Father's Day featured an interview with a man he vaguely recognised from the 'Shawe, a recovering addict who spoke about his abusive upbringing, his subsequent problems with drugs, his own early failures as a parent, and how he was learning with support from the church and social services to be a good father to his two-year-old son. It certainly wasn't the kind of thing Albert had expected.

'So, what did you think?' Penny asked after the service had ended. 'Was it as bad as you expected?'

'Well,' he replied, giving her a knowing look, 'what I think is that you've invited me for breakfast partly under false pretences. I've got a suspicion that the vicar's enlisted your help in rounding up some of her straying flock. But, to answer your second question, I have to be honest and say, "No, it wasn't as bad as I expected." In fact, it was quite good. If enough people find out about it, it might be a good way for some folk to find their way back to church. It's a bit like sneaking in after the service has started and sitting at the back hoping nobody notices you while you finish your breakfast! One up to the vicar in thinking of the idea.'

Penny was obviously pleased with her morning's work and decided not to pursue her evangelistic goals any further for the moment. They went out to the garden where they drank coffee and chatted for twenty minutes until it was time to make the Zoom call to Reggie at half past eleven. As soon as they came back into the kitchen, Albert began to feel nervous at the prospect of what he was about to do. How would he know what to say? What if he said the wrong thing and caused offence to a disabled person? It wouldn't be the first time he'd unintentionally used a phrase that was fine thirty years ago but was now quite politically and socially incorrect. His anxiety was obvious to Penny, who patted him on the hand as they waited for Reggie to respond to the invitation to join their online meeting.

'Don't worry. I know he'll like you. And he'll do most of the talking. You'll just need to listen a bit more attentively to catch everything he's saying. If he's on his usual form, you might even have a job getting a word in edgeways. One of his carers will join the call for him in just a minute.'

As soon as Reggie's face appeared on the screen, his delight at seeing his mother was obvious. Albert sat off to the side, just out of range of the camera on the laptop, observing the interaction between mother and son with interest. Reggie's involuntary tremors and occasional writhing movements revealed that his was a fairly severe case of cerebral palsy. But his speech, though laboured and breathy, was not too difficult for Albert to understand provided he paid close attention.

It was five minutes before Penny was able to get Reggie to pause so that she could introduce the person by her side. She beckoned Albert to come closer to her so that the camera could pick him up.

'Reggie, I want to introduce you to Mr Stridemore, my new friend. His first name is Albert and he has an allotment where he grows lovely healthy vegetables and a garden where he has the most beautiful flowers I've ever seen. I think you'll really like him. Would you like to say hello to him?'

'Hello, Mr Stridemore. It's very nice to meet you.' Despite his courteous greeting, Reggie was looking puzzled. 'But you're quite old. I didn't think that my mother had friends as old as you.'

The guileless simplicity of Reggie's words made Penny smile and won the immediate affection of her new friend. Albert had always been most comfortable with people who came straight to the point and didn't beat around the bush.

'I suppose I am quite old,' he replied with a chuckle. 'I think your mother is so kind that she's nice to people however old or young they are.'

Reggie seemed satisfied with that answer and felt no need to pursue the subject any further. He had more pressing matters to discuss.

'I eat a lot of vegetables and I really like flowers, Mr Stridemore. What kind of flowers do you grow?'

Penny watched and listened for the next quarter of an hour as Albert responded to one question after another until Reggie had explored matters horticultural to his satisfaction.

'My word, Reggie,' Albert concluded admiringly, 'you do know the names of a lot of flowers.'

Reggie would have responded by moving on to his equally extensive knowledge of vegetables had not his mother decided that his interrogation of Albert had gone on long enough for a first encounter and that she should take over again.

'I'm sure Mr Stridemore will talk to you another time about his vegetables,' she assured him, as their conversation drew to a conclusion. 'And I promise you that when this nasty virus has gone away, we'll spend an afternoon together at his allotment. You'll enjoy that and he'll show you all kinds of interesting things.'

That seemed to strike the perfect note on which to end, and after Reggie had told his mother several times how much he loved her and thrown a kiss in her direction, they said goodbye. Penny logged out, closed her laptop and looked at Albert approvingly.

'You did very well for a man who doesn't like Father's Day. Maybe your paternal skills are not quite as rusty as you thought. I think you deserve a cup of tea for your efforts. So why don't you make yourself comfortable? Go and sit in the lounge with your feet up and I'll bring it through to you. I'm sure you could do with a rest after that cross-examination by my son.'

Albert was glad to accept the offer. He settled himself in the leather armchair in the lounge, put his feet on the padded footstool he'd used on his previous visit and thought about the conversation he'd just had with Reggie. It had stirred into life feelings that were always just below the surface, however hard he tried to keep them buried and out of his thoughts. His own son Jeffrey would be fifty-two now, no longer a young man, not even just middle-aged if you really thought logically about that phrase. He would be well into the second half of his life – if he was still alive. That was the hardest burden of all to bear. Hopefully Jeffrey's involvement with drugs had been nothing more than a youthful dalliance that he would have grown out of. But what if his father's harsh treatment had pushed him further down that road and into an early grave?

Of course, Albert could make excuses for how he'd reacted. It had been difficult trying to bring up his son on his own. But that was no justification for his failure as a parent. Penny had been left on her own too. And she'd raised a disabled son with all the pressures that must have put on her, while still having a demanding career in education. If only he could go back to that fateful day in 1988 – thirty-two long years ago – when he'd ordered Jeffrey to leave the house. And he *had* tried to find him, without success. But it was too late now. And regret, as he'd reminded himself before, was a wasted emotion.

'You're looking pensive, Albert.' Penny put down the tray and poured the tea. 'Or maybe you're just tired. Reggie's questions can be quite exhausting if you're not used to talking and listening to him.'

'I guess it's a bit of both. The conversation with Reggie was worth the effort. It was a privilege really. Just to see how much he loves you and how proud you are of him. The downside is that it reminds me of my own failure to be a good parent when my son needed me most. I rejected him when I should have been giving him the kind of love and support you've given to Reggie.'

He reached to pick up his teacup and accidentally knocked over the contents of the milk jug.

'Now that's ironic,' he said, quickly mopping up the milk from the tray with a paper napkin. 'No use crying over spilt milk, as they say.'

'No, there isn't,' Penny responded with a laugh. 'And you can't get the milk back into the jug. But sometimes, like you're doing now, you can do something to mop up the mess. Anyhow, enjoy your tea. Then you can have a bit of shut-eye while I see to one or two things.'

Just as she'd suggested, he drank his tea and dropped off to sleep. It was far from being a peaceful afternoon nap, however. In his dream, he was looking out of the window at Jeffrey, who was a toddler again, playing by himself in the garden. But suddenly he saw that the boy was casually plucking the heads off some of his best flowers, throwing them up in the air and laughing happily as he watched them fall to the ground. In a fit of rage, Albert dashed out and struck the child on the head with his fist, knocking him unconscious to the ground. Overcome with remorse, he tried desperately to revive his son. But, whatever he did, there was no sign of life. As he looked at the child's lifeless body, he felt himself trembling. He woke to see Penny standing over him and gently shaking him to rouse him from his sleep. Thank God, it was only a dream.

'Goodness me, you *were* in a deep sleep.' There was a note of alarm in her voice. 'Are you alright? You're not feeling ill, are you?'

It took a moment for him to compose himself enough to tell her that he'd just been having a bad dream. He assured her that he wasn't unwell.

'I'm sorry to disturb you,' she continued, clearly relieved. 'But I've just had a Zoom call and they're asking for you. They must have found out about our bubble somehow. It might be a good idea to give your face a wash and comb your hair. Whoever it is, you don't want to talk to them looking like you've just got out of bed.'

He asked who the caller was, but Penny shrugged and said she'd never seen the man before. Could be anyone, she speculated. But since the call was for him, he was the one to find out. Still only half awake and a little irritated, Albert made his way to the bathroom, wondering why she hadn't just asked whoever it was for a name and why, if they wanted to speak to him, they'd called *her*. It didn't make sense. But before he could reason that through, he had a brief moment of panic. What if word of their bubble had got round and people were assuming his motives were not entirely pure? By the time he made his way to the kitchen he was feeling confused, embarrassed and even more irritated at the prospect of having to talk to this mystery caller.

He sat down at the kitchen table and glanced at the face of a man in his early fifties on the computer screen. It certainly wasn't anybody he knew. He offered a brusque 'hello' and waited for the man to answer. And as he waited, he wondered why the man staring back at him was beginning to look oddly familiar. And he couldn't understand why, instead of returning his greeting and explaining his business, the man seemed to be struggling to speak. Then – the oddest thing of all – the man began to cry. That was when Albert knew who the man was. That was when *he* couldn't speak either. That was when *he* began to cry too. He was looking at a face he hadn't seen since 1988. A face he never thought he would see again. It was the face of his son. *He was looking at Jeffrey.* His irritation was replaced by a terrible fear that he was still asleep and still dreaming.

'How… I mean… Is it you…?'

He could neither find the words nor put them in any kind of order to construct a sentence. But the monosyllabic sounds he was uttering seemed to be making some kind of sense to the man at whom he was looking, who was nodding in response and saying over and over again, 'Yes, it's me… It's Jeffrey…'

180

Penny eased her chair alongside his and put her hand on his arm.

'Albert,' she said very quietly. 'I think I owe you an explanation before I leave you alone to talk to your son.'

The expression on Jeffrey's face as she came within range of the camera was enough to make it clear to Albert that this wasn't the first time they'd spoken to each other. She must have set this whole thing up! That explained her confusing message when she'd woken him up a few minutes ago.

'I could tell from our conversation back in May how much you regretted what had happened and how much you really wanted to see Jeffrey. It occurred to me that if he was anything like you, he might have the same stubborn sense of right and wrong that caused you to react as you did when you asked him to leave. Maybe, I thought, that was what was keeping him from contacting you. And I wondered whether, if I could find him and speak with him, I might just be able to clear the logjam that's kept you both apart for so long.'

Albert could see that Jeffrey was smiling and nodding in agreement with everything she was saying. It was obvious that his son had willingly cooperated with her attempts to bring about reconciliation. That set his tears flowing again. Penny paused to allow him to compose himself again before she continued.

'I called in some favours from a couple of old students of mine who run an agency that, among other things, has developed some expertise in tracing people. It makes it a little easier, of course, when the person you're looking for is called Stridemore, and it didn't take them too long to find him. There aren't too many people with that surname in the world. To cut a long story short, I took the liberty of contacting Jeffrey and found, just as I'd suspected, that he was a chip off the old block and just needed a little encouragement to make contact.'

She patted him on the hand and stood up with a look on her face that showed she was satisfied with the results of her work.

'Now you know what I've been up to. And, from what I've just been witnessing, my efforts have been more than rewarded. But it's time I left you two to talk. You've got a lot of catching up to do.'

When she'd left the kitchen, both men tried to say sorry so often that the sound kept cutting out. Jeffrey, who was clearly accustomed to the challenges of videoconferencing, took the initiative.

'Dad, I didn't have the sense to listen to you when I was still at home, so the least I can do now is to let you speak first. I promise I won't interrupt. Just give me a wave to let me know you've finished what you want to say. Then I've got a lot to tell you.'

Albert paused to wipe his eyes and blow his nose. He was still not entirely sure that he wouldn't suddenly wake up and find it was all a dream.

'This is a day I didn't dare to hope for,' he said, slowly shaking his head. 'But it really is you. I can see that. Now that I've had the chance to look at you properly. You look older. Though you would do after more than thirty years. And your hair's a bit thinner, of course. But your eyes give you away. They've still got that same look that I used to get annoyed about. You've had it since you were a little boy. You know, as if you didn't quite believe what I'd just told you and you were about to question it. I saw it that night when I ordered you out of the house. But I was so convinced that I was in the right and you were in the wrong that I didn't even give you the chance to question what I'd said. I really am sorry. I wish I could go back and change things. I can't do that, but I can make sure I listen to you now.'

There was no reply from Jeffrey and Albert wondered if he'd said the wrong thing and upset him. Then he remembered that he should have gestured that he'd finished what he wanted to say.

'Oh yes... I'm supposed to give you a signal!' He held up his hand. And, just to be sure that Jeffrey had got the message, he added, 'Over to you now.'

'The first thing I need to say is that you shouldn't be too hard on yourself.' Jeffrey leaned forward so that his face filled the screen. 'It was as much my fault as yours. At least you did what you did from the best of motives. I was just young and arrogant and wouldn't listen to advice. And I never did get to Canada. That turned out to be just a pipe dream. Or, in my case, I guess, a cannabis dream.'

'So that's why I didn't have any success in trying to find you,' Albert broke in. 'You were never there!'

'I'm afraid not.' Jeffrey gave a wry smile. 'I'm sorry about all your wasted efforts. Penny told me about your attempts to get in touch. It wasn't as easy to get into Canada as we thought. And looking back, I'm not even sure if we ever really intended to do it or if we'd just talked about it. No, I never left the UK. And I've been living in a village just outside Bristol for the last fifteen years with my wife and two kids…'

'You've been in the UK all this time!' Albert was too taken aback to remember that he should signal before interrupting. 'And you're married with a family? Goodness me. I can't believe it. It's too good to be true.'

'I sometimes think that myself,' Jeffrey laughed. 'Even more so now that we're in touch again. But it wasn't always as good as this. You need to know that you were right to be worried about the cannabis thing. I know for a lot of young people it can be a passing phase that doesn't lead to anything worse. But that wasn't how it went for me. That's the not-so-good bit of my story. Let me start at the beginning…'

His account of the first few years after he'd left home did not, as he'd warned his father, make for pleasant listening. The friend with whom he was supposed to be going to Canada was using hard drugs, and it wasn't long before Jeffrey himself began experimenting with cocaine and heroin. For a few years he managed to hold down a job, labouring on building sites, restricting his drug habit to what he told himself was 'just a recreational thing for weekends'. But by the mid-nineties it had become an addiction that had taken over his life and seemed set to destroy him.

'I'm not making excuses,' he said. 'And I'm certainly not blaming you. I wasn't a kid who didn't know any better. I was in my twenties, old enough to be responsible for my actions. But I was angry about everything. I was angry at you, angry about dropping out of university, angry about not making anything of my life, angry about the fact that I could see what was beginning to happen to me but that I was powerless to stop. The angrier I got, the more drugs became a way of blocking it out. That went on until the summer of 1996 when, for some reason, I gravitated to Bristol. That's where things got even worse before they got better.'

The part of the story where things got worse was not easy for Albert to hear. Jeffrey had been squatting in a derelict shop in the St Paul's area of Bristol. It had become a gathering point for men and women with nowhere to live and no hope of escape from their addiction. He'd been reduced to begging for food in the streets and sharing needles with his fellow addicts. Residents in the nearby houses, understandably fearful of the risk of fire and disease, resented their presence. The police would move them out regularly and the local authority would have the place boarded up. But within a few days, the same sad group would force their way back into the building and the cycle of occupation and eviction would start again.

'We'd been living like that for almost a year when it happened. I don't know what his real name was, but everybody called him Metal Mickey. He wasn't into drugs. Alcohol was his thing. I don't think I ever saw him sober. He was in an even worse state than most of us there. The police found him on the waste ground just outside the squat one morning. His head had been beaten in with a paving slab. They rounded up five of us who'd been seen drinking and shooting up with him just after midnight. We were all suspects. But none of us could remember anything about what had happened. In the end, they had to let us all go. They never found out who'd done it. But it was a wake-up call for me. It wasn't just the fear that I could end up like that. It was the terrible thought that any one of us could have been the one that did it. We were all so drugged up that we wouldn't even know.'

Albert could see that the recollection of those events was painful for his son. He waved at the screen.

'You don't have to tell me any more. It must have been terrible. And I don't want to make you go through it all again.'

'You're right. It was terrible. But it was the thing that stopped me in my tracks, though I needed a bit of help. There was a Salvation Army place opposite the squat that used to do a hot meal for homeless guys like us once a week. There would usually be seventy or eighty of us lined up, waiting for them to open the door at four o'clock every Sunday afternoon. One of the women who served up the food took a particular interest in me for some reason. Said she'd got a son about my age. The week after Mickey died, I was in a real state. She talked to me for a while. Told me that her husband worked in addictions and that if I really wanted to get clean, to be outside the Sally Army building at ten o'clock the next morning and she'd make sure he was there to meet me. I'm not sure how I managed to get myself up in time, but I was there right on the dot. They must have pulled a few strings because they got me straight into the residential rehab programme where he was on the staff. Those twelve months weren't easy and there were times I wondered if I'd make it. But it set me on the right path. When I completed the programme, knowing that I'd worked on building sites before, they got me a job with a small local building firm. And that's the work I've done ever since. I decided to branch out on my own about fifteen years ago. I've got my own business now. Nothing spectacular. Just me and three guys I employ doing home extensions, that kind of thing. But it gives me a decent living.'

He stopped to drink from a glass of water and Albert took the opportunity to chip in again.

'Here I am all these years trying to picture you somewhere on the other side of the Atlantic and all the time you've been less than 200 miles away. What is it they say? So near but so far away.'

'I know. And I feel really bad about not getting in touch. I thought about it – more than once. And Natalie – that's my wife – nagged me about it. But I'm afraid my pride got in the way. I'd always tell her, "He told me to leave. It's up to him to get in touch and put things right." I really regret that now.'

'Well, you're not the only one with regrets. That's all in the past. But I want to know about my daughter-in-law and my grandchildren.'

'Well, they're right here and they want to meet you too.'

Jeffrey made room for the dark-haired woman who came alongside him.

'Hi, I'm Natalie,' she said with a smile. 'Like he told you, I've been nagging him for years to get in touch with you. It's good to see your face. And I'm really looking forward to getting to know you. Here's our two kids. Ethan's seventeen and Abigail's fourteen.'

'Hi, Granddad.' It was Ethan who was speaking. 'Nice to meet you. Dad said I should tell you that when I've done my A levels, I'm hoping to go to college and do a BSc in Horticultural Science and Management. He says I must have inherited my interest in the subject from you. Mrs Finch told Dad about your allotment. I'd love to see it when we come up to visit you.'

After his initial shock at realising the Zoom call was from Jeffrey, Albert had just about succeeded in getting control of his emotions. But seeing and hearing his grandchildren for the first time completely breached his defences. He was relieved when Penny, who he guessed had been listening outside the door, tiptoed back into the kitchen and sat beside him.

'Jeffrey, I think maybe your dad's had as much good news as any human being can cope with for one day. Why don't we let him come back down to earth and you can talk again tomorrow?'

'You're right,' Jeffrey responded, wiping his eyes with his handkerchief. 'It's been a lot for all of us. Before I go, Dad, I just want to say we'd drive up and see you straight away if we could. But I tested positive during the week for the coronavirus. I've been doing some work in a house where there are four kids in the family. Seems I caught it there. I'm fine. It doesn't feel much more than a mild dose of flu. But it means we're all having to stay in isolation at the moment. We'll sort out a time to come up as soon as we can. Talk to you tomorrow.'

The four members of the family leaned into the camera and waved goodbye, leaving Albert staring at the blank screen and wondering yet again if it was all a dream.

'Why don't we take a walk before dinner?' Penny suggested. 'It does funny things to your head if you sit and look at a computer screen too long.'

'Yes, we should,' Albert agreed, getting up from his chair. 'I don't know what it's done to my head, but I know that any more surprises like that would be bad for my heart. A bit of exercise will do me good.'

They walked together, saying little, content just to take in the sights and sounds of a sunny Father's Day afternoon in Irmingshawe Park: couples strolling hand in hand, families eating together at picnic tables, children running around happily in the safety of the play area, groups of noisy teenage girls talking and laughing with each other, boys playing football and hoping that at least some of the girls were watching them. Albert had passed through the park almost every day for the last ten years and he'd long appreciated the opportunities offered to the community by this green space. But never had it looked to him as it did at this moment. For so many years he'd been an observer, distanced from the people around him and excluded from their simple pleasures by a sense that he was destined to be alone. Now he was included and it felt good. Without thinking what he was doing, he took hold of Penny's hand. She smiled at him and they walked on in the sunshine.

# 13
# 4th July 2020
# Guilt and Gratitude and Going Forward

The sky was overcast and a light but persistent rain was falling on the 'Shawe. The unpleasant weather did nothing to dampen the spirits of those hardy souls who donned their overcoats, put up their umbrellas and came out of their houses to greet the start of the weekend with an enthusiasm they hadn't felt for some time. The daily statistics were showing that across the nation there was a steady decline in new infections and deaths from the coronavirus, and the general opinion was that things were definitely getting better.

'We're through the worst of it,' folk told each other confidently. 'With a bit of luck, things should be back to normal in another month or two.' Best of all, after fourteen long weeks, the restrictions imposed by the government had been loosened and the country was emerging, albeit tentatively, from lockdown. From today they could eat a meal in a restaurant, have their hair cut by a hairdresser, watch a movie in the comfort of a cinema, spend a whole day at a theme park, head off for the weekend at a campsite, or avail themselves of one of the many attractive cut-price deals being offered by hoteliers who were anxious to entice them back to their establishments.

Of more immediate interest to some of the 'Shawe's residents, however, was the long-awaited reopening of the George and Dragon. Despite the permission of the government and the pleas of his thirsty customers, Mick Lafferty, the landlord, had resisted the temptation to open his premises at six o'clock in the morning. He knew his clientele too well to make such an early start. The last thing he needed was a pub filled with customers who hadn't had a proper night's sleep and who'd be drinking on an empty stomach. But he was delighted to welcome the dozen men whom he recognised as his faithful regulars and who were waiting impatiently in the rain when he unlocked the doors just as the clock behind the bar struck ten. All he had to do now was to pull the pints – which, even after his long layoff, he knew he could do without thinking – and remind his patrons to observe the social distancing regulations, which he suspected would be a lot more difficult than pulling pints after they'd had a drink or three.

The pub had been open for half an hour when a man about six feet tall, carrying an old shopping bag and wearing a belted light-brown overcoat and a flat cap pulled over his eyes, came through the door. The landlord immediately recognised the new arrival's distinctive gait and the heavy tread of his solid leather brogues on the wooden floor.

'Good morning, Mr Stridemore,' Mick called out in unfeigned pleasure at the sight of yet another customer. 'I didn't expect to see you so soon. You usually honour us with your company on a Friday evening. But I guess you've worked up a thirst over these last few months. So is it the usual – a half-pint of bitter? And are you OK with me taking a note of your name? It's the new rules for pubs. A bit of a nuisance I know, but rules is rules.'

'Oh no, it's too early in the morning for me,' Albert replied, as he turned towards a customer sitting by himself in the corner. 'I've just come in to pick up some keys from Dave here. Betty Merton, the care home manager, asked if I'd mind tidying up the garden for them. The firm that does it on contract has two of its employees isolating with the virus and can't get anybody out to them today.'

Dave Aitken was the part-time maintenance man at the Park Care Home and he was more than happy to pass on the keys of the hut in which the garden furniture and tools were stored. Saturday was his day off and he was relieved that he wouldn't have to head into work and leave his long-awaited pint half-finished. Besides which, gardening wasn't his thing, particularly on a grey, damp day like today.

'You're a gentleman, Albert,' he said, handing him the keyring. 'You sure you don't want to stop for a swift one before you go back out into the rain?'

Albert declined the offer. Betty Merton had seemed a bit stressed, he explained. He ought to get round there straight away and do what he could to help to make her feel a bit better.

'She's really exhausted,' Dave agreed. 'It looked at first as if they were going to get through this time without too many problems. But in the last month they've lost five of the residents to the virus. The place is in its own lockdown. The care staff have been great. They've been sleeping there at nights. None of them has been home with their families for weeks now. And nobody's going in or out. I haven't even been allowed into the building since I got back after coming off the ladder last month when I was cleaning the guttering. I've filled in my time doing whatever I can out-of-doors – servicing the van, painting the garden furniture, relaying one of the paths – that sort of thing. I know Mrs Merton's been worrying about the garden getting untidy, so I'm sure she'll appreciate your help with that as much as I do.'

Albert went back out into the rain and set off for the Park Care Home feeling troubled by what he'd just heard. He'd been aware of the impact of the coronavirus on care homes around the country and the disproportionate number of deaths that had taken place in them. But he'd been so caught up with other things that he'd paid little attention to something that had been happening right here on the 'Shawe. Besides his regular trips to his allotment and his ongoing involvement with GGOSH, his mind had been increasingly focused on his unexpected reunion with Jeffrey and his blossoming friendship with Penny Finch. While other people were content to set their sights no higher than 'getting back to normal', he was contemplating a future that went far beyond what he'd regarded as normal for more than half his life. After thirty years he was a father again. A grandfather, too! And, though he hardly dared put it into words, he was allowing himself to hope that after half a century on his own there might be the possibility of a relationship that would be more than just a close friendship.

He felt guilty and grateful in equal measure. Guilty that he'd given so little thought to a group of the most vulnerable people in the community, some of them younger than he was, for whom this time had brought increased loneliness, severe illness and, in the worst cases, death itself. And guilty about what he felt was the cavalier attitude of too many people around him who were assuming that the virus had all but disappeared and that they could lower their guard. He feared for the consequences of such carelessness.

But he was also grateful. Grateful that, in his seventy-sixth year, he was fit and healthy with meaningful work to do. Grateful that he had two very good friends in Binu Patel and Penny Finch, and a recently discovered family that he could call his own. He hadn't forgotten that life was unpredictable and that happiness could disappear as quickly as it had come. But he was discovering as never before that unimagined blessings could appear just as suddenly. In the past he'd learned to bear life's losses without falling into despair and giving up. Now he knew he must learn to receive the gifts life offered without being crippled by the fear that they might be snatched away at any moment.

The clue to living like that, he kept reminding himself, was right there in the advice he often gave to people who would ask him how he could walk as far as he did at his age. The trick, he would explain, was to stop worrying about the distance or the uneven terrain. Just walk one mile. And then do it again and again and see how far you can go and where it will take you. In fact, he would add, if they were still listening, it's even easier than that. Don't even think about walking a mile. Just take one step, then another, then another. You'll go further than you thought you could go and, on the way, you'll see all kinds of interesting things.

By the time he reached the care home and unlocked the door of the lean-to where the gardening tools were stored, the rain had begun to ease and the sun was slowly emerging from behind the passing clouds. The grass was still too wet for him to mow the lawn, but he could clean up the flowerbeds and leave the place looking a little tidier. He hung his coat on a hook on the back of the door, put on the overalls he'd been carrying in his shopping bag, and took just a hoe and broom from the array of tools leaning against the wall.

In less than an hour he'd turned over the soil, pulled up the weeds and swept the pathways. The job wasn't quite to his satisfaction, but it was the best he could do in the time he had available. When he'd put everything back in its place and locked up the lean-to, he tapped on the window of the office where he could see Mrs Merton sitting at her desk.

'That's tidied things up a bit,' he called through the glass. 'I'll come back when it's drier and cut the lawn for you. But how are you doing? This can't be an easy time for you.'

He could see when she came over to the window just how tired she was. And he thought she looked noticeably thinner than when he'd last seen her.

'Albert, you're a gem. It worries me if I think the place is looking neglected, especially at a time like this when I'm trying to keep everybody's morale high. But I'm doing OK, thanks. Hopefully things will get a little easier in the next week or so and we can go home and sleep in our own beds.'

They chatted for just a little longer about how emotionally and physically exhausting life had been for the staff, the toll it had taken on the residents and the grief of families who'd been unable to comfort their elderly, dying relatives in their final hours. And once again Albert could sense that combination of guilt and gratitude that had been with him all morning. But Mrs Merton had things to do and it was time for him to go home and have some lunch.

He was about 100 yards from his front door when he noticed a red Range Rover pull up and park in front of his house. It wasn't a car he recognised but he could hazard a guess as to why it was there. The longer lockdown had gone on, the more people had got into the habit of ordering goods online, and the greater the number of deliveries that were being made on the 'Shawe at all times of the day. At first it had been mainly vans and trucks bearing the logos of the big courier companies, but increasingly packages were arriving in unmarked private vehicles. He couldn't remember ordering anything so it must be for Gary and Eileen next door. Since he knew they'd both gone back to work and wouldn't be at home, he quickened his step to get there in time to take the box into his house for them. The driver, who'd obviously seen him coming, got out of the car to wait for him.

'If it's for next door, you can leave it with me,' Albert said, as he walked up the path and fumbled for the key in his pocket.

'Well, that's not the kind of greeting I expected.' The delivery man was walking slowly towards him. 'I come all this way with my family to see you and you think I'm just another guy dropping off a parcel.'

Albert stopped, turned around and dropped his key in surprise. It was Jeffrey!

'We've all been given the all-clear. No coronavirus in the family. So we thought we'd celebrate coming out of quarantine by paying you a surprise visit.'

Being reunited with his son in a videoconference a few days before had been a very special moment for Albert. But seeing him here, just a few feet away and smiling at his father's obvious confusion, was something else entirely. The scene he'd imagined so often in the past sprang to mind – himself as the waiting father and Jeffrey as the returning prodigal. But it was no longer a mere figment of his imagination. *It was real.* Like the father in the parable, he would have run down the path and embraced the son who'd been lost but was found. But the rules, though they'd been relaxed on this very day, still insisted on social distancing. So they stood two metres apart and looked at each other, hardly able to believe what was happening. They'd cried when they'd seen each other on a computer screen on Father's Day. But now there were no tears. There was only laughter. Long, deep laughter that reminded Albert of happy times when Jeffrey was a little boy who thought his dad was the cleverest and funniest man in the world.

The rest of the family, who'd been watching the drama of father and son's reconciliation play out before them, emerged from the car and lined up one after the other behind Jeffrey to be greeted by Albert – first his daughter-in-law, Natalie, and then Ethan and Abigail.

'Now, before we do anything else,' Natalie said, breaking into the momentary silence and pushing her way to the front of the line, 'the kids and I want to see your garden. Your son's been telling me that it was always the best in the neighbourhood. And from the look of your perfect lawn, I'm guessing it's just as good now.'

Albert proudly led them to the little patio at the back of the house where they stood and looked in admiration at his perfectly ordered colourful flowerbeds. Jeffrey remarked that the garden was even better than when he'd last seen it – a verdict with which the others readily agreed with a round of applause, despite the fact that they were viewing it for the first time. That set them laughing again until Jeffrey called for order while he said something suitable for the occasion.

'Now, this is a great day for the Stridemore family. We four agreed when we decided to drive up that it calls for a party. And since the sun's doing its best to shine, I think we should set up a table right here in the garden where we can enjoy your handiwork while we eat. We knew you wouldn't have anything ready for us since, of course, you weren't expecting us to turn up like this. So we've brought the food and drink. We'll fetch it out of the car in just a minute or two.'

Ethan and Abigail, who hadn't got up in time for any breakfast before they'd set off from Bristol just after eight o'clock, and who were not overly impressed by their dad's efforts at public speaking, were keen to get on with it. But Jeffrey had something else he needed to say before he came to the end of his impromptu speech.

'There's just one more thing I need to add. I took the liberty of calling Binu Patel as we were driving up and inviting him to join us for lunch. He's going to try to get out of the shop for half an hour and come round. If we stay in the garden he won't be breaking any rules.'

Albert was delighted that his son had remembered his oldest friend, though he felt just a twinge of regret that he hadn't thought of a new friend who might have been invited.

'Oh, and I almost forgot...' The faint smile on Jeffrey's face suggested that his reference to his poor memory wasn't exactly truthful. 'I hope you don't mind, but I also invited Mrs Finch to join us. After all, without her efforts we might never have managed to find each other. And she's clearly become a very good friend in a very short time. She seemed keen to accept the invitation. She even insisted on bringing some of her specialities that she said you liked, just to add to the food we've brought.'

As if on cue, Penny Finch came walking round the side of the house with a basket filled with some of her home-baking. Albert was glad to see her, not simply because she had indeed become a good friend, as Jeffrey had said, or even because of the delicacies she was carrying, but also because her arrival distracted the attention of the others from the fact that he was blushing again.

Chairs were carried out from the house, food was set out on a couple of tables, a bottle of wine was opened, a toast was proposed to the blessings of family, and then, as the clouds parted, leaving the sun to shine unobstructed from a clear blue sky, they shared the meal together. They shared it as such a meal should be shared – with more talking than eating, more listening than talking, and the sound of laughter punctuating the proceedings at regular intervals. They honestly confessed their regrets for the mistakes of the past. They gladly expressed their pleasure in the joys of the present. They eagerly anticipated all that the future might bring. And they sought to preserve the moment for ever by taking photographs and movie clips on their smartphones.

The arrival of Binu Patel half an hour into the proceedings served only to heighten their awareness that this was a very special occasion and one they should never forget. An occasion in which the elation of the Stridemores at being reunited with each other intermingled with their sympathy for the Patel family in their loss of Pranav without any sense of incongruity. It was Binu who, as he so often did, captured the truth they were experiencing.

'My sadness should not spoil your joy,' he said, quietly accepting their condolences. 'And your joy does not offend my grief. There must be room for both in life. And often both at the same time.'

It was four o'clock in the afternoon when they cleared away what little was left of the food. Albert sat talking in the garden with Jeffrey and Binu and Penny Finch. From time to time he looked through the kitchen window at Natalie, Ethan and Abigail doing the washing-up. It was a moment that filled his heart with a happiness he'd never before experienced. These were the six people who mattered most to him in all the world and he could imagine no greater pleasure than having them together in his home. He watched them talking and laughing while they worked together to leave everything clean and tidy and thought that he would be happy to sit there all day. Jeffrey, however, had other ideas. He summoned his wife and children back into the garden.

'I must say that this is a happy picture of domestic bliss. And I've never seen Abigail and Ethan help with the washing-up so willingly. But I hope you won't mind if I have my dad all to myself for a few minutes. We haven't had the chance to talk to each other alone since we got here. And I think it's time for us to start making up for all those father–son conversations we've missed over the years. So, please excuse us while we take ourselves off for a chat. And don't worry, Dad,' he added, leading Albert to the bottom of the garden, 'I'm not going to ask you to lend me any money.'

They stood facing each other, both of them remembering the times when such a stance had been the prelude to so many tense confrontations between them. Albert tried to say again how sorry he was about the past hurts and the lost years. But Jeffrey shook his head and held up his hands.

'No, Dad. Don't. We both made mistakes, but we're both a lot older and a little wiser than we were back then. And we've got a lot of time to make up. So let's not waste that time with any more regretting or apologising. There's too much for us to be grateful for and we don't want to let guilt for the past spoil all that. You lost your son. Now you've got him back with interest – he comes bringing a daughter-in-law and two grandkids. I walked out on my father. Now I've got a dad who has the respect of everyone who knows him.'

'You're right, son.' There was an unmistakable wistfulness in Albert's voice. 'But I just wish all this hadn't happened so late. I wish I could look forward to another thirty or forty years.'

'Well, I guess none of us knows how long we've got ahead of us. And that's really what I wanted to talk to you about before we hit the road. You can tell me to mind my own business if you want. But I need to say it to you. Don't let your age keep you from taking every opportunity you have.'

He looked at his father with an expression of love and admiration that transported Albert back to the time when he was a young, single father to a happy, trusting little boy.

'You know, that's just how you used to look at me when you were a child.'

'Yes, I guess I did,' Jeffrey said thoughtfully. 'I used to do it when I needed a bit of reassurance, to feel safe. And I think you need a bit of that now. I've only been here a few hours, but I can see there's something special between you and Penny. Something more than just good friends. And I think your head may be telling you that you're being an old fool and that it's too late. Or that you're just a retired postman and she's had a very different kind of career.'

Albert could feel himself blushing yet again, but Jeffrey didn't seem to notice. Or if he had, he'd chosen to ignore it and press on with what he wanted to say.

'Now I'm in danger of sounding like one of those agony aunts in a magazine. But seriously, Dad, do what your heart tells you on this one. You're a good man and you deserve another chance to find the love that was taken away from you so early in life.'

'Thanks, son. I appreciate what you've said. Let's see what happens in the next little while. It's a bit scary being given a second chance, as you put it, when I'd thought that my life was fairly predictable.'

'Well, I'm sure you'll do what's best. And I promise you that I won't interfere or offer you any more of my advice. I'm a builder, not a counsellor, and I'll stick to my trade from here on in.'

They stayed where they were for another minute, both of them grateful for this conversation and reluctant to draw it to a conclusion. Before they returned to the others, Jeffrey had something else he wanted to say.

'By the way, on the subject of second chances, I just wanted to tell you that Natalie and I have linked up with a church near where we live. Ethan started going to some of the things they do for teenagers with one of his mates. Sounds like the kind of thing you went to in your youth. Then I did some work for them, building an extension that gives them space to expand what they do in the community. They seemed pretty pleased with the job and they invited me to the opening ceremony. Even asked me to make a short speech. I hate doing that kind of thing, but it got a round of applause. I guess it mustn't have been too bad. And, even more important, they paid the invoice in good time. We went quite a few Sundays until the coronavirus meant they had to cancel their services. They've been doing an online service since then that we've listened to most weeks. It's the first contact of any kind I've had with religion since the folk in Bristol got me into the rehab centre. So I probably owed church a visit. But I wondered…'

Albert looked at him questioningly and waited for him to finish what he was saying.

'To be honest, Dad,' Jeffrey added tentatively, 'I wasn't sure whether I should tell you about it. I mean… after what happened to you in Bornaby, I guess you must be suspicious of anything to do with church.'

'Oh, that was a long time ago now. You've got to do what's right for you. And Penny's got me listening to the online service from St George's on a Sunday morning. So who knows what might happen? I still have long talks with Binu about life, where we're headed and what might be waiting for us.' He looked at his son and grinned as they rejoined the others. 'Well, you can't help taking an interest in all that kind of stuff when you get to my age.'

The visit Albert would always remember had come to an end. He stood with Binu on one side and Penny on the other as Jeffrey and Natalie and Ethan and Abigail got back into their car to drive home, all four of them assuring him that next time they came it would be to take him back with them to visit them in their home near Bristol. Binu and Penny drew just a little closer to him as his family drove off, and together they watched until the red Range Rover reached the end of the street, turned on to Irmingshawe Road and disappeared from sight.

Binu smiled at him.

'You are a very fortunate man, Albert. And I am grateful to you for allowing me to share this wonderful day with you. But I am not forgetting my customers who are needing my services. My part-time assistant will be going home soon. I must hurry back to my shop.' Then he added with a chuckle as he set off, 'But I am leaving you in the capable hands of your bubble chum. I am sure she will take care of you.'

The warm afternoon sun had disappeared behind the clouds and the evening had quickly grown chilly, but Albert asked Penny if she'd mind sitting in the garden with him for a little while, 'just to complete a perfect day'. He put on one of his tweed jackets and she wrapped herself in a warm blanket.

'We look for all the world like a postcard I once saw of Darby and Joan,' she joked, as they settled themselves on the bench at the bottom of the garden. 'Your neighbours will be wondering why on earth these two old people are sitting out in the cold.'

'Well, let them wonder. To be honest, I was hoping we looked a little more romantic than that. Because I want to ask you a question.' He was suddenly afraid that his courage might desert him. His heart was beating loudly as he forced himself to speak. 'Actually, I wanted to ask you if you'd consider marrying me.'

She clasped her hands, tilted her head to one side and took a long look at him before she replied.

'Now, that is an interesting question.' She paused. It was only for a moment, but it was long enough for Albert to worry that he'd done the wrong thing. Then, to his relief, she gave him a beaming smile. 'Of course, my answer is yes. I'd be very happy to marry you. But I've got a question for *you*. Why did we have to come out and sit in the cold before you asked me?'

'The honest answer is that I thought it would be easier for you just to get up and walk away if I'd got it wrong and the answer was no. I was afraid if I asked you when we were indoors you might feel trapped.'

'You really are a gentleman, Albert Stridemore. Come over here and put your arms round me. I need someone to warm me and I want to give you a kiss.'

Gary and Eileen at number 79 were in their kitchen when they heard their next-door neighbour calling to them from his garden. But they were delighted to abandon the washing-up when he told them his good news. Standing on opposite sides of the garden fence, the two couples raised their glasses as Albert proposed a toast to future joys and wedded bliss. It was, he had no doubt, the perfect end to a perfect day.

# 14
## 12th July 2020
## Considering Covid-19

A *strange* time. That was the phrase most people were employing to describe the period since the beginning of lockdown back in March. And Albert would nod and agree whenever he heard it. It was undeniably 'a strange time'. Different in so many ways from anything he'd lived through in his seventy-five years on earth. But as the weeks and months had passed, it became an increasingly less-adequate description of the life of Albert Stridemore in the time of the coronavirus pandemic. Yes, it *was* a strange time. But it was also an *eventful* time. The most eventful time of his entire life.

He'd met a very attractive woman and, before he realised what he was letting himself in for, he'd found himself enlisted in her project to encourage the residents of the 'Shawe to eat more healthily and become a little more self-reliant by growing their own vegetables; he'd been initiated into the hitherto unknown world of digital technology in which sending emails and videoconferencing had become part of his regular routine; he'd supported his oldest and dearest friend through the loss of his only son and the pain of bereavement; he'd appeared on the local television news which had made him – at least for a few days – something of a minor celebrity in the eyes of his neighbours; he'd recognised the reality of racial prejudice and joined the thousands marching through the city in support of the Black Lives Matter movement; he'd become one half of a social bubble and inspired the proprietor of Patel's General Store to coin a new phrase – 'bubble chums'; and he'd been reconciled with his son Jeffrey after thirty years, a reunion that had brought with it the added blessings of a daughter-in-law and two grandchildren he hadn't even known existed. So much had happened to him in such a short time and in what had seemed at first to be the most unpromising circumstances.

Most surprising of all in this eventful time, his marriage to Penny Finch was scheduled for the first Saturday in August. The Reverend Olivia Smithers had agreed to conduct the ceremony at St George's and the reception would take place in the garden of number 5 Irmingshawe Road with a guest list limited to family and close friends in keeping with government guidelines. If someone had predicted such an occurrence at the beginning of the year, he would have dismissed them as crazy.

But what was happening right now would have been almost as impossible for anyone to foresee. It was, he reflected as he entered the studio, all the fault of two very persuasive women. Ten days earlier, Jacqui Aldred had been back on the 'Shawe with her cameraman to do the follow-up feature she'd promised on the progress of GGOSH. As she'd done on her first visit, she'd interviewed Albert about his role in the project and had been impressed, not only by the practical help he was giving to people in the community, but also by the no-nonsense way his answers to her questions got right to the point without a hint of waffle. So impressed, in fact, that she'd recruited him for an upcoming programme she'd be presenting. They'd got together a panel to reflect on what lessons could be learned from the impact of Covid-19 in the region, she explained. There would be a doctor who'd been working on the front line, someone from the university to explain the science behind the pandemic, a historian to help viewers get a sense of perspective on the last few months, and a theologian to answer from a faith perspective some of the big questions about life that people were asking.

'It's an impressive line-up,' Jacqui added. 'But we think it still lacks something. It needs another person on the panel, someone who *isn't* an expert, someone with just good old-fashioned common sense, someone who represents the ordinary man and woman, someone who's just rolled up their sleeves and tried to help in this crisis. Someone like you, Mr Stridemore. So, what d'you think? Are you up for it?'

Albert had immediately protested that he wouldn't be right for that kind of thing. Answering a few questions in an interview was one thing, though even that was a bit of a stretch for him. But being part of a panel with the kind of people she'd just described was quite another. He'd be way out of his depth. The answer was no, and he wasn't budging from that. He would have stuck to his guns had not Penny joined in the conversation.

'Jacqui, he underestimates himself,' she interjected. 'I think he'd be just right for what you want. He'd bring a bit of practical wisdom. Don't let him off the hook.'

He'd been well and truly caught in a pincer movement where further resistance would be in vain. So, despite his initial reluctance, Albert Stridemore – allotment-keeper, retired postman and soon-to-be-bridegroom – was about to appear on a live Sunday morning television show that would be going on air in less than fifteen minutes. He wondered if his fellow panellists could tell just how tense he was feeling as they touched elbows with each other, a form of greeting he found difficult at any time, but particularly awkward with a woman who was more than half a foot shorter than he was. The strange contortions involved in the action did, however, break the ice and ease his nervousness when it became obvious that everyone else was finding this substitute for shaking hands as ungainly as he was.

He even felt himself beginning to relax when they took their seats behind a long, semi-circular table with their chairs placed exactly two metres apart and Jacqui Aldred took up her position, standing just off to the side, from where she would facilitate the discussion. She chatted casually, setting everyone at ease, asking a few simple questions and allowing the sound technician to check the volume levels. And, just before they went on air, she made a point of introducing Albert to the others and referring to what she called 'his really innovative project on the Irmingshawe estate'. When the red light went on to indicate that they were now live, he was relieved that it was beginning to feel a little less like a visit to the dentist for root-canal surgery and a little more like the kind of exhilarating fairground rides he'd enjoyed in his youth.

As the introductory music faded, the presenter stepped forward and spoke to camera.

'Good morning. I'm Jacqui Aldred and this is *Considering Covid-19*, where we've gathered together a group of people to talk about life in this time of pandemic, how we can make some sense out of what's been happening, and where we might go from here. We're grateful that many of you have already sent in questions. So many of them, in fact, that it would be impossible to answer them all individually in the time we've got. But what we've done is to sift through them all carefully and make your questions the basis for our discussion this morning. So, without further ado, let me tell you about our guests.'

As she introduced the other contributors to the show, listing their impressive credentials, Albert wondered why he'd allowed himself to be talked into this and what, if anything, she'd find to say about him. Growing healthy vegetables on his allotment for the last decade after forty years of delivering letters in fair weather and foul wasn't something to be ashamed of. But it did rather pale into insignificance when set against the achievements of this distinguished company. Jacqui Aldred didn't seem to think so, however, when she came to him.

'And last, but by no means least, our panel is completed by Albert Stridemore. Mr Stridemore is a retired postman and a keen gardener with a well-deserved reputation on the Irmingshawe estate, where he's lived for more than fifty years, for his skill in growing prize-winning vegetables. He has a key role in an imaginative and innovative project we've featured twice on our local evening news programme in recent months. GGOSH – *Giving and Growing on the 'Shawe* – was launched in the early days of lockdown and has helped residents in that neighbourhood to become more self-reliant and to develop healthier lifestyles by growing some of their own food.'

Albert smiled gratefully and tried to look more confident than he felt, though he hoped that, if the camera was on him, the make-up that had been applied before the show to prevent his forehead shining under the television lights would also disguise the perspiration he could feel trickling down his brow.

'Let me start with you, Professor Nora Ronson.' Jacqui Aldred turned towards the petite, unprepossessing woman with whom Albert had had such trouble touching elbows. 'As the historian on the panel, I'm going to invite you to have the first word. I'm guessing that the current pandemic isn't the first to occur. Can you set what we've been living through in some kind of historical context for us?'

Professor Ronson confirmed that there had indeed been a number of similar pandemics throughout history. Between AD 165 and 180, what was known as the Antonine Plague, possibly an outbreak of smallpox, had taken the lives of more than 4 million people. In the middle of the sixth century, the Plague of Justinian had killed around five times that amount. And the bubonic plague in the fourteenth century – the one that everyone knew as the Black Death – was reckoned to have resulted in the deaths of anything from 70 to 100 million people, around 20 per cent of the world's population at that time.

'Since then,' she went on, 'there have been a number of cholera pandemics. Then there was the terrible flu pandemic after the First World War. Historians differ on the number of fatalities, but it was anything between 20 and 50 million. Far more than died in the war that had just ended. And, of course, in our own lifetime, we've had things like Hong Kong flu and Asian flu and SARS and Ebola. And I haven't even mentioned yet the HIV/AIDS outbreak that took so many lives.

'So you're absolutely right when you say that this isn't by any means the first pandemic the world has faced. And it won't be the last. The big difference now is that modern medicine has lulled us into a false sense of security and we've assumed – wrongly, as we now know – that such events are a thing of the past. Provided, of course, that you're lucky enough, as we are, to live in a part of the world with a functioning health care system.'

Professor Ronson's concluding comments led into a discussion on the demands placed on the National Health Service at the height of the crisis. Albert saw his opportunity to chip in. After all, he thought, you don't need to have a string of letters after your name to appreciate the work of doctors and nurses and the other front-line workers in our hospitals.

'I'm probably the oldest person in the studio. If I've got my dates right, I'm three years older than the NHS. So for almost the whole of my life I've benefited from our health service. But I can remember my grandmother talking about how difficult it was for ordinary people to get

213

proper medical care or even to see a doctor before the 1950s. And I think that if these last few months have taught us anything, it's been that we need to hold our politicians to account. Make sure that they allocate sufficient funds to ensure the future of the NHS that's looked after all of us during this time.'

His comments met with unanimous approval from the others around the table and drew a response from Dr Aliza Dhariwal, a consultant virologist.

'Mr Stridemore is absolutely right. And I know he speaks for most people in Britain today. Those times when people have stood out in the street and applauded what we've been doing have been really appreciated by all of us on the front line. But if we want the NHS to continue to provide world-class medical care, it'll need more than applause. It's not just the politicians who need to support us. It might well be that we'll all need to pay a little more in our income tax over the coming years.'

Again, there was general agreement with what Dr Dhariwal had said. But she hadn't finished. Now there was a passion in her voice that bordered on anger.

'And I need to add this. Despite all that we saw on our TV screens when the crisis was at its height, I'm still not sure that everyone understands what a serious disease this is. Too many of us still seem to think it's only the very old who get really sick or die and that for the rest of us it's nothing worse than a mild dose of flu. Coronavirus kills young and healthy people too. *It's a deadly disease and it hasn't gone away.* It's already killed more than 40,000 people in this country and it'll be with us for a long time yet. This is a time to remind people that we all need to work together to keep this thing at bay. We need to keep washing our hands regularly, to wear a mask in public places, to observe the social-distancing guidelines. It's too late for too many by the time they're admitted to hospital or have to be taken into intensive care. Doctors and nurses like me don't want to be the heroes pulling people back from the brink of death. It's the responsibility of us all to save lives. We'll only succeed with all of us pulling together. And, if we don't, we'll all fail together.'

This time the response was a thoughtful silence from the other panellists, and Jacqui Aldred was experienced enough as a broadcaster to allow a moment of quietness before she moved on.

'Maybe this is the right time to turn to you, Dr Linford Williams. As we've just heard, this virus has brought bereavement and suffering to so many families. And it's raising some of the big questions that perhaps we manage to avoid when everything's going smoothly. You teach theology to students at university and you're also on the leadership team of one of the biggest churches in the city. What does religion have to say to us in a time of pandemic? I've heard of some religious people suggesting that this is all part of God's judgement on us. Would you agree with that?'

Albert, who'd heard the same thing and had asked himself what kind of God would send a pandemic that killed people indiscriminately to get their attention or punish them, was anxious to hear the reply. He took the pen and paper that had been set in front of each contributor and got ready to take notes.

215

'Well, thank you for starting with an easy one!' Linford Williams held up his hands in mock horror and laughed. 'Seriously, I'm more than happy to answer that question with a resounding no. I should just acknowledge before I go any further that, as a Christian, I don't have any authority to speak on behalf of other faiths. Though, having said that, I believe there's a lot of common ground between people of different faiths. But let me respond to your question as briefly as I can.'

The gist of his answer was simply that while there were stories in the Old Testament of God sending plagues as a way of punishing the ancient Israelites and calling them to their senses, he did not believe that was the main thrust of either Jewish or Christian teaching.

'Of course, I think we're all beginning to realise that the pandemic we're facing now *does* challenge us to change direction, *does* tell us that it's time to start building a more just society. It's shining a light on the terrible truth that across the world and even in our own country there are millions who lack the bare necessities of life. And it's those people – the poor and the underprivileged and the dispossessed – who are facing the greatest suffering at this time. That in itself would be enough to convince me that a good God wouldn't send a plague that inflicted the greatest hurt on those who were the least responsible for the injustices and inequalities that are all round us.'

Delighted at what he'd heard and without even thinking about what he was doing, Albert banged his fist on the table and shouted, 'Hear, hear!' Jacqui Aldred smiled at him. But noticing that the woman wearing headphones and standing next to one of the cameras didn't appear to be quite so pleased with his instinctive reaction, he quickly clasped his hands and tried to look as if nothing had happened. Unperturbed by the interruption, Linford Williams pressed on with his argument.

'The big overarching truth that I encounter in the Bible is this... We live in a good world, a world of beauty and wonders, a world that exists not as a result of blind chance, but at the will of a loving Creator. At the same time, however, it's a world that exists distinct from its Creator, a world that's been spoiled and marred by something dark and evil, a world in which that darkness and evil can and does infect all of us. So it's a dangerous world, a world where bad things can and do happen, a world in which people are free to do what's good, or to do evil. That tension between good and evil is shot through every page of the Bible and is there in every story it relates. And though some believers find it frustrating and try to fill in the gaps, it doesn't tell us a whole lot about where that darkness comes from or how it got into the warp and woof of the world. The question with which it constantly confronts us, if we seriously engage with it, is not, "Where did evil come from and how did it get here?", but, "What's to be done about it and how can we overcome it with good?"'

He paused momentarily and took a sip of water from the glass in front of him. Albert, suddenly concerned that his microphone might be picking up the noise of his pen scraping across the paper as he scribbled down some notes, glanced at the woman wearing the headphones. To his relief, she wasn't looking in his direction. And Linford Williams was picking up where he'd left off.

'When we get to the New Testament – and this is what's distinctive about Christian teaching and what governs my perspective on life in general and on this pandemic in particular – we are confronted, not with an angry deity who sends plagues and disasters on the world to punish people, but with a loving God who comes into the world in Jesus, who gets right down into all the pain and suffering and evil, who takes it all on Himself and transforms it into what is good and life-giving. That, of course, is why the cross has always been the great Christian symbol. It's not that we're obsessed by cruelty and death. Quite the opposite. It's because we see hope in the worst of things and in the darkest places. For people who believe what I believe, the resurrection of Jesus is not just a historical event. It is the definitive sign that good triumphs over evil, the unequivocal promise that ultimately all wrongs will be put right and everything will be made new.'

'That was quite a *tour de force*,' Jacqui Aldred responded. 'It's not hard to tell that you're a preacher, Dr Williams. And I can certainly understand how what you're saying would bring comfort and hope to believers. But, of course, you're looking at the world from a faith perspective.'

She took a step towards the stocky, bearded, grey-haired man who was sitting to her left and who'd been listening closely to what Linford Williams had been saying.

218

'Let me turn to you, Professor Jurgen Schneider. You're a scientist and a leading epidemiologist. I'm guessing that, as a scientist, you take a much more hard-nosed approach to things. But before you address the issues, can you just explain in layman's terms what an epidemiologist actually does and why it's so important at a time like this?'

'Yes, I can do that in just a sentence or two. Epidemiology is the study of disease as it impacts a population. It's about investigating what has caused a particular infection, where it has come from, the factors that are allowing it to spread, and how it can be controlled and its effects minimised. I usually describe what I do as a bit like being a detective. Except that instead of investigating crimes and arresting bad guys, I'm investigating germs and trying to stop them in their tracks. I start with the facts and work from there. I focus on collecting and analysing and interpreting the data available to us so that we can make informed and practical decisions on how best to protect the health and well-being of the nation at any time. Epidemiology has rightly been called the basic science of public health. It's going on all the time, though most of us are only aware of it at a time like this.'

Albert, who'd half expected that Jurgen Schneider would sound like the stereotypical Teutonic scientist who turned up regularly on popular television comedy, was impressed by his quiet and restrained manner and his ability to communicate in everyday English without resorting to unintelligible scientific jargon. He listened closely while the professor explained that Covid-19 had likely crossed over from animals to humans in a 'wet market' in China and that its progress had possibly been aided by the reluctance of the authorities in that country to acknowledge and alert other governments to the fact that a new and potentially deadly virus had been unleashed on the world. It was good to hear someone present things so simply; he couldn't resist asking a question.

'So, do you think,' he asked tentatively, 'that we'll ever be able to get rid of all viruses and make the world safer?'

'Goodness me, no,' Professor Schneider laughed. 'And we wouldn't want to get rid of every virus. We tend to talk about viruses only when one of them harms us – just like this coronavirus. But here's the interesting thing that most folk never think about. In fact, even scientists like me are just at the beginning of understanding all this. It's a bit complicated, but I'll try to explain briefly and simply. Are you ready for this, Mr Stridemore?'

'It sounds fascinating,' Albert responded. 'But remember – I'm a retired postman who left school at fifteen, sixty years ago. Just make it as simple as you can.'

'Well, I'll do my best. There are more than 100 million types of viruses in our world. And only about twenty of those types are dangerous to humans. The rest are actually important for our survival on this planet. Without getting too technical and going into too much detail, it's important to remember that viruses aren't living organisms. They're just bits of genetic material that act like parasites, attaching themselves to cells. And they play a key role in the ongoing processes of recycling inorganic nutrients that keep the food chain going. Without them, none of us would be here.'

Albert did his best to look intelligent as he tried to get his head around what he'd just heard. He'd never thought about there being such a thing as a *good* virus. That was quite a discovery for him. And Professor Schneider was about to say something else that hadn't occurred to him before.

'Come to think of it, it's one of those places where faith and science can actually find themselves in some agreement. Like Dr Williams said earlier, this is a good and wonderful world. But it's also a dangerous world that can hurt and harm us. That's what his faith teaches him as a believer, and that's what I learn as a scientist observing the processes of nature. I hope that we can also agree that the challenge for us both is to work to alleviate suffering and make the world a safer place.'

Jacqui Aldred had been allowing the discussion to flow without interruption from her. But now Albert could see a glint in her eye as she took a step forward and addressed her words to Linford Williams.

'That's an interesting point that Professor Schneider's just made. But I'm wondering, Dr Williams, if it's really true that religious people are committed to working to make the world better. What I mean is this: if you believe, as you obviously do from what you've said, that in the end everything will come good, doesn't that lead to a kind of fatalism? Doesn't it make people think that since it'll all work out in the end, there's no need to try to change things? I know that at times like this religion can be a source of great comfort to people. But isn't there a real danger that it can also become a kind of escapism from the problems of life? Isn't too much religion just "pie in the sky when you die"?'

Linford Williams' eyes widened and he sat bolt upright as if in shock. Albert wondered if he was at a loss as to how to answer the question. But then his face broke into a smile and he began to stroke his chin in mock contemplation.

'Well, if I were a politician, this is the point at which I'd say, "I'm glad you asked me that." But, honestly, I really am grateful for your question. In fact, I've got two answers that I can give you. The first is that what you've been describing is really a caricature of what Christians believe. The great Christian hope isn't focused on escaping the trouble of the world and going to the peace and security of heaven when you die. We do, of course, believe in what's often called an afterlife, but it's part of something much bigger. What we hope for is not just the survival of individuals. We believe in a future where everything will be made new, restored to the Creator's original design, and where there will be no more pain and suffering and evil. And that brings me to the second answer I want to give you.

'Far from offering an escape, our Christian faith challenges us to work for that glorious future every day. To bring the future into the present, if you like. That's why, in what's often called the Lord's Prayer, Jesus taught his disciples to pray for His kingdom to come and His will to be done on earth, right here and now. And that's why, in many of those pandemics back in history that Professor Ronson reminded us of, long before there was anything like our wonderful National Health Service, Christians were often on the front line caring for the sick and dying. Far from their faith being an escape from reality, it was an incentive to roll up their sleeves and get involved. And that's why, in this present crisis, you'll find Christians working alongside people of other faiths and people of no faith at all to alleviate suffering and make life better for those around them.'

Albert thought that was a good answer, though he'd given up in his efforts to keep notes, and he just hoped that Jacqui Aldred wouldn't come to him for a comment on what he'd just heard. When she immediately picked up on Linford Williams' concluding comments to segue to the next part of the show, he quietly breathed a sigh of relief.

'You certainly make an important point when you refer to people of different faiths serving together with those who have no specific religious beliefs but who are motivated by a concern for their neighbourhoods. Take a look at what's been happening in our region over recent months in response to the present crisis.'

What followed was a five-minute video giving glimpses of the voluntary work being done by people from different ethnic backgrounds and representing different faith traditions and community groups. The last thirty seconds featured a clip from the launch of GGOSH back at the beginning of May. As it drew to a close, Albert could see Jacqui Aldred pointing at him from across the studios and he guessed that he was about to have his moment in the spotlight. He tried to relax and prepare himself for whatever she was going to ask him.

'That was a just a quick overview of some of the good stuff being done all over our region by unsung heroes like

Mr Stridemore who we saw in those closing shots. GGOSH – or *Giving and Growing on the 'Shawe*, to give it its full title – is a food bank with a plus.' She turned to address Albert directly. 'You decided not just to give out food but to help people grow their own and become a little more self-sufficient. It sounds simple enough but I'm sure it must take a good deal of work. Tell us why you got involved and what you've learned from it.'

Albert was quick to acknowledge that at first he'd been a reluctant recruit and that the credit for getting things off the ground went to Penny Finch and the other women who had been working with her. But he took a little more time to say what he'd gained from the experience.

'Well, of course, I've learned what most people learn who get involved in serving others – that it does more for you than for the people you're trying to help. Makes you think about what really matters in life. And I've developed some new skills. I now know how to get on the internet and make Zoom calls. Quite something for an old luddite like me.' His confession caused him to smile before his expression became more serious. 'But I've discovered something about myself that I hadn't suspected. I was remembering the other day that over the years I've invited a lot of folk to come up and have a look at my allotment. And I've always tried to be generous and send them home with a basket full of freshly picked vegetables. But that was all about *them coming on to my patch*. It was like I was the lord of the manor benevolently allowing them to view my estate. It's a bit late, I know, but I'm learning that it's really something I just hold on trust. I have the privilege of tending it, sowing seeds, nurturing plants and sharing what I've learned.'

He felt a sudden flush of embarrassment and he wondered if he'd sounded pretentious and highfalutin in front of people who were far more educated than he was. But the others seated around the table seemed to be listening intently and Jacqui Aldred was looking at him with an expression on her face that suggested she was willing him to say a bit more.

'That's an interesting thought, Mr Stridemore. Do you think there might be lessons in that for your fellow panellists?'

'Hmm… I don't think I'm the best person to be giving advice to people who are far more highly educated than I am.' He hesitated, unsure of how he should answer the question. 'I've been at a church service for the last few Sundays after hardly being in a church building for fifty years. St George's on our estate has been doing an online service. They've decided that since folk can't go to them and sit in the pews, they'll bring the church into our houses. I think there's a lesson to be learned there. Maybe we could all do better at getting alongside folk rather than just asking them to come to us. Showing that we really are all in this together, rather than just telling them what to do. The worst example – and I think it's already done damage to people's trust – was when the Prime Minister's top advisor to all intents and purposes broke the rules and was allowed to keep his position. He wouldn't even apologise for what he'd done. But they're still expecting us to obey the rules. And I'm still angry about that.'

Immediately the words were out of his mouth, he wished he hadn't said them. He was about to apologise when the sound of 'Hear, hear!' coming from around the table made it clear that everyone else on the panel was in agreement with him. And the presenter was obviously equally pleased.

'Well, you've obviously struck a chord there, Mr Stridemore. I'm sure we could have a lively discussion on that topic. But your comments have also set us up nicely for the second half of the show. It's time to go to the phones and hear what some of our viewers have to say to us. So, let's take our first call...'

The rest of the programme ran smoothly and Albert was able to relax and actually enjoy the experience. When it was all over, he thought about catching a tram but then decided to walk the four miles home from the studio. It wasn't just that walking was the healthier option. He needed the time to think. He'd just been on television. He'd just been thanked by Jacqui Aldred for doing exactly what she'd wanted – bringing a bit of balance to what could have been an academic discussion. And he'd just been congratulated by his fellow panellists, one of whom had even told him that he was a 'natural behind a mic' – a comment to which he responded by saying that he was more comfortable standing behind a hoe or a spade.

As he stepped onto the street, he threw back his shoulders, got properly into his stride and smiled at the thought of what he was discovering about the world and about himself at this time. Though he had to admit that it had come only after years of digging!

# 15
# 1st August 2020
# Getting to the Church on Time

Albert and Penny had elected to dispense with the tradition of the bride getting to the church after the groom. They would travel together to St George's, they would then proceed hand in hand up the aisle past their waiting guests, followed by Penny's sister as her bridesmaid and Binu as Albert's best man, and arrive in front of the vicar at precisely one minute after two o'clock. The Reverend Olivia Smithers would greet them, offer a suitable prayer, read a relevant passage from the Bible, lead them through the ceremony, pronounce them husband and wife, and complete the job with the required dignity but with the minimum fuss.

'After all,' Penny said, squeezing Albert's hand when they'd discussed the matter, 'nobody's "giving me away". I'm a mature woman, I'm of sound mind and I'm doing this of my own free will. And, apart from all that, I don't want you sitting at the front fidgeting if I'm two minutes late. I know what a stickler you are for time, Albert Stridemore. So just remember that I'm beside you when we set off from the back of the church. And don't break into your usual stride and leave me scurrying behind you.'

Albert, being Albert, had insisted that they spend a whole afternoon rehearsing their entrance until they were sure they could complete the walk from the porch to the front pew in fifty-seven seconds exactly and at a pace that suited them both.

It was now two o'clock on Saturday 1st August and everyone who should be there was there: Albert's son, Jeffrey; his wife, Natalie, and their children, Ethan and Abigail; Penny's son, Reggie; and, of course, Penny's sister, Camilla, Albert's best friend, Binu, and the Reverend Smithers, all three of whom were waiting and ready to play their part in the ceremony that was about to unfold. But Albert and Penny had still not arrived. Knowing what had happened two weeks earlier, however, the members of the small congregation were not altogether surprised that the start of the service was delayed. And they were prepared to wait...

Dawn had broken over Manchester on Saturday 18th July revealing overcast skies and heavy rain. The kind of morning that people in sunnier southern regions of England assume to be typical of the climate in the north-west of the country. While Mancunians often objected that it was an unfair assumption, even the most loyal of them would have been forced to confess that this was the latest in a month-long sequence of such wet days. But the gloomy weather could do nothing to dampen the spirits of Albert and Penny. The bubble chums, as they happily referred to themselves, were enjoying a leisurely breakfast in the kitchen of number 77 Park Avenue and chatting about their plans for the day two weeks hence when they would exchange life in the temporary protection of a fragile bubble for the permanent and solid state of holy matrimony.

Penny had arrived just after half past eight, expecting to sit down to nothing more elaborate than a bowl of cereal and some fruit, only to find that Albert was busy preparing what he described as 'a proper fry-up', and the kitchen was already filled with the aroma of bacon.

'I promise you I'll do the healthy thing every other morning of the week,' he said, placing the two platefuls of bacon, eggs, mushrooms, fried bread and black pudding on the table. 'But I've been eating a cooked breakfast on Saturdays for the last fifty years. You've been down in London for such a long time you've forgotten the delights of northern cooking. This'll help you feel you've really come home.'

It was, she had to admit as she looked out at the steadily falling rain, the right kind of comforting food for such a damp and dreary day. In fact, it was so comforting and filling that before she'd even started her second cup of tea, she'd dozed off in the armchair. She woke from her nap to the sound of Albert's voice and the touch of his hand on her shoulder.

'I've been reading the paper and watching you for the past twenty minutes. I can't remember when I last felt so contented. I didn't want to wake you, but the vicar's expecting us in less than half an hour and we'd better not keep her waiting.'

The rain was coming down more heavily as they stepped out of the door. Penny was sheltered from the elements by her bright yellow waterproof jacket and a floral-patterned umbrella. Albert, who'd long eschewed the protection of what he dismissively described as 'one of those gamp things', insisted that his trusty light-brown belted overcoat and his flat cap pulled down over his eyes would afford him all the covering he needed from the worst of the weather. He would have done the gentlemanly thing and held the umbrella over his wife-to-be had not the difference in their heights made such a gallant gesture impractical. But he did remember to adjust his step so that she could keep beside him without having to break into a run. The handful of neighbours they passed and to whom they offered a cheerful 'Good morning' could have been forgiven for thinking that they were an unlikely couple. But at that moment, en route to their meeting with Olivia Smithers and under a slate-grey Mancunian sky, they were as blissfully happy in each other's company and as much in love as two young people with all of life before them.

The enterprising vicar of St George's, somewhat annoyed by the decision of the Anglican bishops that churches should not be open for personal prayer during lockdown and intent on continuing to provide pastoral support to her parishioners while staying within the confines of the law and obeying the dictates of her superiors, had erected a gazebo on the stretch of grass in front of the church. The church grounds, being open to everyone, she reasoned, qualified to be considered as a public park, albeit a relatively small one. And the gazebo, being open on two sides, was really nothing more than an open-air venue. Therefore, she concluded, it was perfectly permissible to meet here with anyone who needed her help. Thus far no one in authority had challenged her rationale, and for more than a few residents of the 'Shawe it had become a place in which they could find a listening ear and an encouraging word. Someone skilled with a needle and thread and with a knowledge of the Old Testament had even attached a plain white handkerchief to one of the sides of the gazebo on which were embroidered, in a suitably ornate font, the words *Olivia's Tabernacle*.

It was to this improvised meeting-place that Albert and Penny came at eleven o'clock. The Reverend Olivia Smithers, having conjectured that conversation in a draughty gazebo on a rainy Manchester morning would flow more easily if aided by the stimulus of caffeine, had set out a flask and three cups ready for their arrival. Her assumption turned out to be correct. As they drank the warm coffee, they laughed about the weather and the incongruity of the setting; they talked about life on the 'Shawe and the importance of the presence of the church in the heart of the community; they read through the marriage ceremony line by line, sensing the solemnity of the relationship on which they were about to embark and acknowledging the significance of the vows they were about to make. And then, after a pause while the flask was refilled and the coffee cups were replenished, the two women listened and Albert talked about the hurt that had been done to him so long ago and the chasm it had created between him and the faith he'd once held.

'That's why,' he concluded, 'that apart from Easter Sunday each year, I've not been a regular attender at church.'

'Come on, be fair to yourself, Albert,' Olivia Smithers chipped in with a laugh. 'You could put up a reasonable argument that once a year *is* regular – though it certainly isn't frequent.'

He was grateful for her tongue-in-cheek interjection. She was clearly trying to make this easier for him and he appreciated that. Penny leaned across and took hold of his hand, giving him a look that he recognised as an encouragement to keep going.

'You're right, it hasn't been frequent. And I'm not sure that I fully understand why I turn up one day a year. I don't think it makes me a believer, unless hanging on to the hope that life means something qualifies as some kind of faith. I told my friend Binu not so long ago that my allotment's become a kind of substitute for church. It probably sounds silly to you. Or maybe you'll even decide I'm a terrible heretic and refuse to conduct the wedding when I tell you. But I tried to explain to him that watching the seeds I've buried push their way up through the soil, becoming beans or carrots or whatever, gives me the same feeling...'

He hesitated, unsure of how to continue, concerned that he might be saying the wrong thing, that he might offend the woman who'd agreed to conduct their marriage. But Olivia kept looking at him and mouthed the words, 'Go on.'

'Well... it gives me the same kind of feeling I used to have when I went up to receive communion. You know, a row of growing vegetables is the most ordinary thing in the world, but it's become like a window into the meaning of things. Like bread and wine are just ordinary things – just another stage on from being plants that we lift out of the soil – but they've come to mean something more, something that's impossible to explain in words, something that you need to experience.' His confidence began to drain from him and he hesitated again. 'Oh dear, I'm just an old man talking round in circles. I'm not making any sense, am I?'

'On the contrary, Albert, I think you're talking perfect sense.' Olivia wasn't laughing now, but she was smiling broadly. 'Obviously, being a vicar, I believe that being part of a church and joining with other people in worship is very important. But I know that sometimes people who've been hurt or damaged by church can find that very difficult. And I also know that we encounter God far beyond the walls of a church building. I guess that's why we have the parables in the New Testament. Why, when Jesus wanted people to glimpse what God is like, He told stories of ordinary things He could see in the world around Him. Why some of His most insightful stories are about good soil, about seeds falling into the ground and dying, about harvest time. Why He told His disciples to remember His death, celebrate His presence among them and look forward to His coming by using the produce of the land. Told them do it by drinking wine and eating bread.'

A sudden gust of wind blew one of the empty coffee cups off the table and across the grass. Instinctively, Albert got up and strode across the wet grass to retrieve it.

'It's good to see I'm marrying a man who's fit enough to look after me,' Penny joked as he put the cup back on the table. 'I can look forward to a life of ease.'

'I reckon you're both pretty fit and active,' Olivia said. 'And I know you've got other things to be doing today. But there's one more thing I want to say to you before you go. Albert, you mentioned that you weren't sure if hoping and looking for meaning in life qualified as faith. Well, it's certainly a good starting point. And I wonder if I can encourage you on the next stage of your journey. I'd be very happy to offer communion to you both right now. I can sense from what you said that it's something you've missed. You should still go on looking and listening for God when you're digging in your allotment, of course. But there's no reason why you should feel excluded from a place at the table where so many find meaning and hope.'

It was an offer the couple seated in front of her were glad to accept. And so, as the wind gusted through the gazebo and the rain beat out its steady rhythm on the canvas roof above their heads, the Reverend Olivia Smithers, intent on dispensing grace to the souls of sincere seekers while dutifully observing the prudent guidelines issued by the House of Bishops, gave bread and wine to two people preparing their hearts and minds for the next step in their journey together.

By two o'clock, the wind had died, the rain had eased and patches of blue sky had begun to appear from behind the clouds. Penny had work to do in the kitchen at home, stocking the freezer with more tasty home-baking for their wedding reception, and Albert had decided to take the opportunity to spend the afternoon at his allotment. They walked together along Park Avenue, holding hands and commenting on how pleasant the ordinary things of life were when you had someone to share them with. And when they reached Irmingshawe Road they stopped before they separated and Penny turned left in the direction of her house.

'If anybody's watching us, they'll be wondering why two people of our age are behaving like this,' Penny whispered as they hugged each other tightly. 'My mother always told me that cuddling a boy in public was unbecoming for a young lady.'

'I don't care what your mother said. And I don't care what anyone else is thinking. It's none of their business.' Albert didn't keep his voice to a whisper, just to prove to himself and anyone who might overhear them that he really didn't care. 'And anyhow, the good thing is that we won't need to say goodbye like this for much longer. Soon you'll be Mrs Stridemore and we can do everything together.'

'Well, if you want our guests to have something nice to eat at the wedding, you need to let me go. And you need to get on with whatever it is you've got to do.'

Reluctantly, he did let her go. But he stood for almost a minute and watched her after they parted.

As he turned back and headed across the road and through the park, he marvelled to himself that just looking at someone you loved walk along the street could be a source of such exquisite pleasure. He'd always appreciated the feel and smell of a day in which morning rain yielded to afternoon sunshine and where every growing thing was fresh and green and bursting with life. But this was different. Better than anything he'd experienced before. Life was good; an understanding vicar had beckoned him back into the fellowship of the Church; the future was filled with promise; and in two weeks' time he would marry a woman who, for reasons he would never fully understand, loved him and admired him. No wonder he was whistling again. It wasn't a tune that he could give a name to, but it matched the rhythm of his footsteps and it gave a release to the joy that was filling his heart.

There was a hint of warmth in the sun by the time he reached the allotment and he took time to look around as he pulled on his blue overalls. The adjoining parcels of land were deserted. He could only guess that his fellow allotment-keepers, assuming the inclement weather had set in for the day, had decided to stay indoors. The only other signs of human life he could see were two young lads, one of whom looked to be about ten and the other who could have been no more than five or six, playing on the waste ground on the other side of the wire mesh fence that surrounded the allotments. They waved to him and called out, 'Hello, Mr Stridemore,' and he recognised them as brothers belonging to a family who lived in the next street to his.

He was always intrigued that, despite the recreational ground on the 'Shawe estate with its two football pitches and all the amenities available in Irmingshawe Park, the abandoned stretch of land held a strange fascination for boys. No doubt, the tales they heard from their grandparents of wartime days when the old aircraft factory had stood there gave the place an aura of danger, and appealed to their thirst for adventure. It reminded him of his own boyish fantasies of a life filled with feats of derring-do that would draw the admiration of his contemporaries and win the thanks of a grateful nation. Growing prize-winning vegetables and delivering letters in the rain, it had to be admitted, fell somewhat short of that ambition. But, all things considered, it hadn't been a bad life. And the discoveries of recent days, he gladly acknowledged, far surpassed anything he'd anticipated unearthing at this time of life.

But he hadn't come to the allotment just to stand around and reminisce. There was a job to be done. A job that never failed to fill him with satisfaction. It was time to harvest the potatoes he'd planted back at the beginning of May. He eased his spade from the hook on which it hung, appreciating the pull of its weight on his arms and enjoying the feel of the wooden handle smoothed by years of use. All the gardening manuals he'd read advised that this was a task best done with a digging fork. But a lifetime of careful practice and a simple preference for the first gardening tool he'd ever purchased meant that almost invariably he completed the job without piercing one of the tubers and spoiling the perfection of the buried treasure he was unearthing.

One by one he eased the roots from the ground, removed the potatoes, gently dusted off the soil with the palm of his hand and placed them reverently in the basket by his side. And when he reached the end of the row, he went all the way back again, still on his hands and knees, gathering up the plants and feeling in the soil for any tubers that might have evaded his grasp. Long experience had taught him that failing to remove them would provide a haven for the spores that would bring the destruction of potato blight. He'd never been one to leave a job unfinished.

He pushed the spade deep into the earth until it stood upright, allowing him to grip the handle and lever himself back on to his feet. It was good to stand straight again, to breathe deeply, to feel the muscles in his back relax, to know that another task had been successfully completed. And today, he decided, that would be enough. Today he'd surprise Penny by following her advice to pack up and go home before he got too tired. There were another two weeks before their wedding. Plenty of time to have everything shipshape before he took a week off for their honeymoon in the Lake District. So today he'd deliver as many of the freshly picked potatoes to her house as he could comfortably carry and then go home and have a shower before returning to number 5 Irmingshawe Road for dinner.

He was drawing the spade out of the soil when he heard someone calling his name. It was the voice of a child and it was coming from the waste ground on the other side of the fence.

'Mr Stridemore, my brother's fallen into a hole in the ground. He's stuck in the mud and he can't get out.'

The younger of the two boys he'd seen earlier was shouting and crying and waving frantically, but the older boy was nowhere to be seen. He knew immediately that something was wrong. And he knew that there was no one else around to help.

He picked up his spade, took the keyring from his jacket, grabbed hold of a rope he kept handy in the shed and hurried towards the gate in the fence that marked the boundary of the allotments. It was an entrance that was hardly ever used and it took precious moments for the rusted padlock to yield to the pressure of the key. By the time he'd unlocked it and pushed the gate open, his heart was already pounding and sweat was running down his face. The rutted and uneven ground, still wet from the morning's heavy rain, would have made swift progress over the 150 yards difficult for a youthful cross-country athlete with proper running shoes. For a man in his mid-seventies wearing stout brown brogues on his feet, it was treacherous.

He slipped and fell twice, bruising his face as it hit the handle of his spade, before he reached the sobbing and panicking child standing by the side of a crater. It was about fifteen feet wide and nine or ten feet deep, and he guessed that it had probably been opened up by the ground subsiding as a result of the persistent rain of the last month. He looked in to see the older boy struggling ankle-deep in mud. His first thought was to tie one end of the rope to something that would support him and to lower himself into the hole, but the fence was too far away and there wasn't so much as a bush in sight to which he could attach it.

There was nothing else for it. Putting the rope over his shoulder and holding the spade close to his body, he sat on the ground at the edge of the fissure and allowed himself to slither down the side until he reached the bottom.

'You're alright,' he reassured the distressed youngster. 'I'll get you out. But you need to stand still while I dig around you. We don't want you sinking in any deeper, do we?'

His spirits lifted when his spade hit something solid less than a foot down. Thank God, he was touching rock. This might turn out to be just a bit easier than he'd envisaged. He quickly scraped away the mud, throwing it behind him. His optimism was short-lived. What he was hearing was not the noise of his spade hitting rock, but the sound of metal on metal. His heart missed a beat. And when he looked down at what his digging had exposed – at what they were standing on – his worst fears were realised. He set his spade down as gently as he could and spoke to the boy slowly and quietly.

'What's your name, son?' he asked.

'Billy Turner,' the boy replied, looking up at the man whose face was splattered with mud and running with sweat.

'Well, Billy, it's really important that you do exactly what I tell you. You need to stand absolutely still. As if you're a statue. I'm going to pick you up and get you as high as I can. When I let you go, you need to dig your hands and feet into the mud on the side of this hole and pull yourself up and back onto the ground beside your brother. Do you understand what I'm saying?'

'I think so, Mr Stridemore.'

'And then you and your brother have got to run as fast as you can and tell someone what's happened. Do you understand all that?'

The boy nodded uncertainly, but there wasn't time to go through it with him again. Albert picked him up slowly and carefully and held him as high as he could. Summoning every ounce of strength in his body and praying that what he was doing would work, he threw him towards the wall of the crater. For what seemed like an age he watched as the boy struggled to push his hands into the soil, which crumbled and slithered down under his grasp. Then, just as he was beginning to think that he would slip back down again, Billy Turner managed to get a foothold and clamber out of the hole.

'Now, you and your brother do what I told you,' Albert shouted. 'Don't stop. Just run!'

He looked down at the markings on the hideous lump of rusty metal that had lain hidden deep in the earth for eighty years. He could see clearly what it was and he could guess where it had come from. It was an unwanted present dropped from the night skies by a Luftwaffe bomber in the Christmas Blitz of 1940. He was crying and laughing and praying and remembering. Crying with sheer relief that two little boys with their entire lives ahead of them were running home to the safety of their family. Laughing at the ridiculous thought that if he ever got out of this hole, he'd have a story to tell about something far worse than lockdown. Praying that help might come quickly and he might see Penny's face again. And remembering the hope that the sight of buried seeds springing to life always stirred in him.

He concentrated hard on standing still. But the ground was shifting beneath him. The unexploded bomb on which he was standing was moving. And there was nothing he could do to stop himself from falling. There was a light too bright for his eyes. And then darkness…

It was now twenty minutes past two on Saturday 1st August and everyone who should be there was there. And everyone who was there stood to their feet as the organ sounded the opening bars of 'Thine be the Glory' and the procession led by the Reverend Olivia Smithers made its way slowly from the back of the church. Albert's coffin was brought into the church with Penny Finch walking immediately behind the bearers, flanked by Binu Patel on one side and her sister on the other. Her right hand was placed firmly on the casket in observance of the pledge they had made to arrive together on this day.

Olivia Smithers apologised for the late start to the service, explaining that, as they'd anticipated when the decision was made that the hearse should drive slowly through the 'Shawe on the way to St George's, the residents had lined the streets, throwing flowers and applauding the man who'd lived in their community for fifty years, inspired them for the months of lockdown, and given his life to save two of their children.

In keeping with the government's guidelines for church services, they sang no hymns. Olivia and Penny, who had planned the service with Jeffrey, confessed to each other that they might have been tempted to ignore what they considered to be an unreasonable regulation had they not been aware of Albert's opinion of people who didn't stick to the rules.

But though there was no singing, the brief and simple service was a fitting tribute to the life of Albert Stridemore.

There were prayers that the God of consolation whose Son was moved to tears at the tomb of Lazarus would look on those gathered in St George's on the 'Shawe with that same compassion, give hope to their troubled hearts and strengthen in them the gift of faith. Jeffrey Stridemore read some verses from Paul's First Letter to the Corinthians that offered an answer to the perplexing question of how the dead might be raised to life with the analogy of the hard little seed that is sown in the darkness of the earth but rises with a beauty and a form far beyond that of the thing from which it has sprung. It was, everyone in that small congregation concurred, a passage of Scripture that was singularly appropriate to the manner of Albert's life and the moment of his death.

And Penny Finch delivered a eulogy in tribute to the man who should have been standing by her side at that moment as they made their vows to each other. Her hearers smiled as she recalled his physical presence, telling them that if she closed her eyes, she could almost hear the heavy tread of his footsteps as he came striding up the aisle. They nodded in agreement as she described the character of the man – his uncomplicated honesty, his passion for growing things, his sense of right and wrong, his determination never to wallow in self-pity, his tender conscience and deep regret for the mistakes he'd made in life.

And they listened intently as she listed some of the lockdown discoveries of the man who only a few months before, at the beginning of the year, had assumed that life held no more surprises. They were impressed by his willingness to come to grips with the mysteries of digital technology so that he could more effectively play his part in GGOSH and the food bank initiative; they were amused and astonished at the revelation that when he'd gone a-courting, he'd swapped his favoured tweed jacket and grey flannels for a sweater and a pair of chinos; they were inspired by his courage in facing the lingering racism in his own heart and marching in the Black Lives Matter demonstration; they were heartened by the recounting of his reunion with his son and his first encounter with his daughter-in-law and grandchildren; they were gladdened by his welcome back into the fellowship of the Church; and they were moved to tears by Penny's concluding words of gratitude that together they had discovered it was never too late to find love and to be found by love.

Later that afternoon, as the little company of mourners stood around the open grave and listened to the affirmation of faith in the words of committal, they clung to the hope that Albert Stridemore had now made the great discovery besides which everything else he'd learned in the time of pandemic would pale into insignificance. And Jeffrey told them of the inscription to be etched on the stone that would stand over his grave.

ALBERT STRIDEMORE
3rd January 1945
18th July 2020

*a man who*
*walked many miles*
*sowed good seeds*
*and gave his life for others*

*I tell you truly that unless a grain of
wheat falls into the earth and dies,
it remains a single grain of wheat;
but if it does, it brings a good
harvest.*
*John 12:24 (J B Phillips)*

It was, they agreed, a fitting epitaph for an ordinary man who had lived through an extraordinary time and made some life-transforming discoveries. They were honoured to have been part of his story, they would treasure his memory, and they would try to follow in his footsteps as they walked through a beautiful but dangerous world.

# Resources

**Epigraph**
https://www.christianitytoday.com/ct/2020/may-web-only/martin-luther-plague-pandemic-coronavirus-covid-flee-letter.html (accessed 20th July 2020).


**2**
https://www.timeanddate.com/weather/uk/manchester/historic?month=1&year=2020 (accessed through April-August 2020 to double check weather on any particular day).

https://www.iwm.org.uk/history/the-manchester-blitz (accessed 6th August 2020).

https://www.express.co.uk/life-style/garden/1259976/allotments-can-i-go-to-my-allotment-during-lockdown-coronavirus-gardening (accessed 27th May 2020).

http://www.downthelane.net/vegetable-garden-year/year-index-page.php (accessed throughout April-August 2020).

https://www.bbc.co.uk/news/uk-52011928, transcript of Boris Johnson's address to the nation 23rd March (accessed 1st April 2020).

5
https://www.thesun.co.uk/news/11321408/what-time-queen-speech-coronavirus/ (accessed 10th April 2020).

9
https://www.theguardian.com/politics/2020/may/25/dominic-cummings-press-conference-leaves-questions-unanswered (accessed 25th April 2020).

10
https://www.manchestereveningnews.co.uk/news/greater-manchester-news/thousands-protesters-flocked-city-centre-18376153/ (accessed 29th June 2020).

13
https://www.instituteforgovernment.org.uk/explainers/coronavirus-lockdown-rules-four-nations-uk (accessed 8th September 2020).

14
https://www.weforum.org/agenda/2015/11/are-viruses-actually-vital-for-our-existence/ (accessed 30th July 2020).

https://www.cdc.gov/csels/dsepd/ss1978/lesson1/section1.html (accessed 1st August 2020), epidemiology.

*Also by Chick Yuill:*

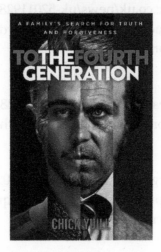

Zander Bennings' writing has brought him a lifestyle his parents and grandparents could never have imagined. But when he is confronted with the cold reality that his success is built upon a lie, he is plunged into a desperate search for truth and forgiveness.

Delving into his family's past, through the battlefields of World War One and down the three generations before his own, he discovers that the men of his family have each been forced to embark upon this same unsettling quest.

Tracing their lives, and those of the women who held the family together, Zander discovers the search is not in vain, and that while family ties can be broken, they can never be truly severed – even to the fourth generation.

*Instant Apostle, 2020, ISBN 978-1-909728-26-4*

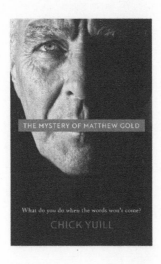

Meet Matthew Gold: wealthy, successful and secure – but totally alone. Afflicted from childhood by a crippling stammer, words have been his greatest problem. But, as his talent as a writer of detective fiction emerges, words become his greatest passion. He might struggle to speak, but on the pages of his novels his slick-talking private eye knows all the answers and can always find the words to illuminate every mystery.

But what happens when life itself becomes a mystery you cannot solve? What do you say and what can you do when words come to an end?

*Instant Apostle, 2019, ISBN 978-1-909728-65-3*

When the caretaker of St Peter's finds that the church has been broken into early on the Saturday morning after Christmas and that the elderly intruder is still in the building and kneeling at the communion rail, no one is quite sure what to do.

But the confusion caused by the sudden arrival of this unexpected visitor is as nothing compared to the impact of his continuing presence on the church and the town. As his identity becomes clear and his story unfolds, long-hidden truths emerge, and life in Penford can never be quite the same again...

*Instant Apostle, 2018, ISBN 978-1-909728-87-5*

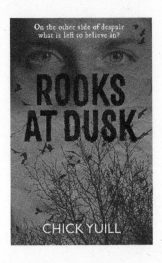

Where can a man find grace when he no longer believes?
Ray Young has been married for almost thirty years. But
his once vibrant faith, like his marriage, is steadily fading,
and relations with his only son Ollie are increasingly
strained.

Facing this looming crisis of faith, Ray begins an affair,
only for Ollie to discover his father's infidelity.
Confronted by his actions, Ray has one chance to rescue
the life that is crumbling around him. But when tragedy
strikes, it seems all hope of redemption is gone…

*Instant Apostle, 2017, ISBN 978-1-909728-65-3*